The Alien

Even the book morphs!
Flip the pages
and check it out!

Look for other **ANIMORPHS**® titles by K.A. Applegate:

the andalite chronicles

The Alien

K.A. Applegate

AN
APPLE
PAPERBACK

SCHOLASTIC INC.
New York Toronto London Auckland Sydney

Cover illustration by David B. Mattingly

ISBN 0-590-99728-9

12 11 10 9 8   8 9/9 0 1 2/0

Printed in the U.S.A.   40

First Scholastic printing, July 1997

For Michael

The Alien

PROLOGUE

Before Earth . . .

<Prepare for return to normal space,> Captain Nerefir said in thought-speak.

I was on the bridge of our Dome ship. It was an amazing moment. I had never been on the bridge before. I'd always been stuck in my quarters, or up in the dome. It was an honor to be on the battle bridge with the full warriors, the princes, and the captain himself.

It was because I was Elfangor's little brother. An *aristh* like me, a warrior-cadet, wouldn't have been on the bridge otherwise.

Especially not an *aristh* who had once run into Captain Nerefir so hard he'd fallen over and ended up bruising one of his eye stalks. It was an accident, but still, it's just not a good idea for lowly cadets to go plowing into great heroes.

But everyone loved Elfangor, so they had to tolerate me. That's the story of my life. If I live two hundred years, I'll probably still be known as Elfangor's little brother.

We came out of Z-space or Zero-space, a realm of white emptiness, back into normal space. Through the monitors I saw nothing but blackness dotted with stars. And there, just ahead of us, no more than a half-million miles away, was a small, mostly blue planet.

<Is that Earth?> I asked Elfangor. <I didn't realize there was so much water. Can you get Old Hoof and Tail to let me go down to the planet with you?>

<Aximili, shut up!> Elfangor said quickly. He looked slightly sick and cast a dubious glance at Captain Nerefir.

I guess I had been thought-speaking a little loudly. Elfangor was worried that War-Prince Nerefir might have overheard. But I was sure I hadn't been that loud. I mean, I really didn't think that —

<Old Hoof and Tail, eh?> Captain Nerefir said. <Is that what they call me?>

Elfangor shot me a poisonous look. <I'm sure this *aristh* didn't mean any disrespect.>

I think my brother would have liked to throw me out of the nearest airlock right at that moment.

Slowly Nerefir turned his two main eyes toward me. He was a frightening old Andalite. A great warrior. A great hero. Elfangor's idol. <Ah, it's the ruffian. The wild brat who knocked me over.> He nodded. <Old Hoof and Tail, is it? Well. I kind of like the name.> He slowly winked one eye at Elfangor. <I suppose we'll have to let the ruffian live.>

Suddenly . . .

<Yeerks! We have a Yeerk mother ship in orbit over the planet!> the warrior at the sensor station cried.

<They're launching fighters! I count twelve Yeerk Bug fighters,> another warrior cried. <They're on an intercept course. They'll be in firing range in twelve Earth minutes.>

Captain Nerefir turned his face and his main eyes toward my brother, while his stalk eyes kept watch on the monitors. The humor was gone from his face. <Prince Elfangor? It is time. Launch all fighters.>

But Elfangor hadn't waited for orders. He was already halfway out the door. My tail banged into the doorway as I plowed after him.

<Get to the dome, Aximili,> Elfangor said.

<But I want to fight!> I said. <I can fly a fighter as well as —>

3

<Do not argue with me, Aximili. *Arisths* do not go into battle. You are not a full warrior yet. Go to the dome. You will be safer there.>

<I don't want to be *safe*,> I said. But a warrior, even a warrior-cadet, has to obey orders. Elfangor was my brother. He was also my prince.

I could hear the thought-speak announcements coming from the bridge:

<Yeerk Bug fighters closing fast.>

<We are entering the outer-gravitational field of the planet.>

Elfangor and I came to a pair of drop shafts. Warriors were zooming down, heading for the fighter bays. I would have to go up to reach the dome. The upward drop shaft was empty.

It made me angry. Everyone was fighting but me. When it was all over, Elfangor would be even more of a big hero, and I would still be the little brother. The child.

Elfangor hesitated for just a moment before rushing on. He arched his tail forward. I reached forward with my own tail, arching it up over my back. We touched tail blades.

<You'll have your chance to fight, Aximili,> my brother said. <Very soon your fighter will fly side by side with mine. But not in *this* battle.>

<Yes, my prince,> I said, sounding very stiff and formal. But as he turned to enter the drop

shaft, I couldn't let him go thinking I was mad at him. I said, <Hey, Elfangor? Go burn some slugs.>

<That's the plan, little brother,> he said with a laugh. <That is the plan.>

It was the last I saw of him.

He disappeared down the drop shaft. I went upward to the great dome. The dome was the heart of our ship. It was a vast, round, open plain of grass and trees and running water from our home planet, all covered by a transparent dome.

I was alone there. The only nonwarrior on the great ship. The only one without a battle to fight.

I could see the blue planet above me, hanging in a black sky. It had a moon, just a dead ball of dust. But the planet looked alive. I could see white clouds swirling. Its yellow sun's light sparkled off the vast oceans.

This planet was known to be inhabited by a reasonably intelligent species. We had learned a little about them in school.

My main eyes were drawn to the brilliant flares of engine exhaust as our fighters lanced toward the onrushing Yeerks.

I was far from the battle bridge now, beyond the range of their thought-speak. I heard nothing in my head. And my ears heard only the sound of a gentle, artificial breeze ruffling the leaves of the trees. I stood on blue-green grass and watched tiny pinpoints of light as the battle was joined in orbit above the blue planet.

And then . . . I felt it. A tremor that rolled through my mind. A wave of coldness . . . a premonition. Like a waking nightmare.

I turned my stalk eyes away from battle, toward the dead moon of the blue planet. And there I saw it. A black shape against the gray-white light of the moon. A shape like some twisted battle-ax.

<Blade ship . . .> I whispered. <A Visser's Blade ship!>

Our fighters were all away. Our Dome ship had massive weapons, but the Blade ship was fast and maneuverable. Too fast!

The warriors on the battle bridge had no choice. They had to separate the dome in order to be able to fight. I felt a grinding, crunching sensation as the dome was released to drift free of the main line of the ship.

Then . . . silence as the dome floated free.

Slowly, the rest of my ship rotated into sight. Without the dome it looked like a long stick, with the huge bulge of engines on the far end, and the smaller bulge of the battle bridge in the middle. They were trying to turn to meet the Blade ship.

Too slow.

The Blade ship fired!

<NO!>

Dracon beams, bright as a sun, lanced through space.

The ship fired again. Again. Again.

An explosion of light! A silent explosion like a small sun going nova.

The ship . . . my ship . . . blew up into its separate atoms. One huge flash of light, and a hundred Andalite warriors died.

WHUMMPPPFF!

The shock wave hit the dome. It was translated into sound. The grass beneath my hooves slammed up at me. A terrible rattling, shaking, heaving.

<Ahhhh!>

My knees buckled and I fell to the grass. Everything was spinning! Wildly, out of control! I could feel the artificial gravity weaken. The stabilizers had failed.

The dome was falling. Falling out of orbit.

The dome slid down the gravity well. Down toward the blue planet. Red-hot glowing atmosphere turned the sky above me to fire. Emergency engines kicked in with a loud WHOOSH!, but they could only slow the descent, not stop it.

The dome hurtled at shocking speed down and down and down through the atmosphere. Down toward the sparkling sea.

Crrr-UUUUUSSSSHHH!

The dome hit water! Boiling, steaming water

rushed over the dome. I was sinking! Sinking beneath the ocean of the blue planet. I was powerless. Terrified.

Alone.

After an eternity, the dome crunched heavily onto the ocean floor. Looking up, I could barely see the surface of the water a hundred feet or more over the top of the dome.

I climbed shakily to my four hooves. I was standing on a vast, open plain that was a piece of my own planet. A blue-green park, hidden deep beneath an alien sea.

And there I waited for weeks. I sent out thought-speak cries to my brother. I knew he would save me . . . if he still lived.

But in the end, it was not Elfangor who found me. It was five creatures from the planet. Five "humans," as they call themselves.

They were the ones who told me of Elfangor's last minutes of life. He had broken Andalite law and custom by giving these humans the power to morph. I was shocked, but tried to hide it.

And they had witnessed Elfangor's death. His cold-blooded murder, by the Yeerk overlord: Visser Three.

Visser Three, who slaughtered my helpless, wounded brother.

Visser Three, the only Yeerk ever to infest and control an Andalite body.

Visser Three, known to all Andalites as the Abomination. The only Andalite-Controller.

He had killed Elfangor, and I had inherited a terrible burden. By Andalite custom, I would be required to avenge my brother's death.

Someday I would have to kill Visser Three.

CHAPTER 1

E*arth* . . .

> The first thing an Andalite may notice about humans
> is that they walk around on only two legs. It is very
> strange to see so many creatures balancing that way.
> But, despite this, they seldom fall over.
> — From the Earth Diary of Aximili-Esgarrouth-Isthill

My full name is Aximili-Esgarrouth-Isthill.

My human friends call me Ax. I am a young Andalite. I have four legs. I also have two arms. And I have a tail.

I am told that I look like a cross between a deer, a scorpion, and a human. I've seen deer in the woods, and I don't agree. For one thing, they have mouths and I don't. And they have only two eyes, while I have four.

As for scorpions, I've only seen pictures. There is some resemblance, when it comes to the tail. An Andalite tail is also curved upward and tipped by a very sharp blade.

As an Andalite, I have the power to morph. It's not something we're born with — it's a technology. But we invented it, and we are the only race in the galaxy that has it.

Except for my human friends, that is.

They can morph, too. But it's thanks to Andalite science. And thanks to the fact that my brother broke our own laws to give them this power.

The one great problem with morphing is the time limit: two Earth hours.

That time limit was the problem as my human friends and I set about on a particular mission. It was a mission that required careful planning and careful timing. It was a mission full of risks.

We were going to a movie.

"So, here's the deal, Ax," Marco explained. "You can watch the first hour of the movie. But that's it. We can get you to the mall theater, and you watch for an hour. Then we have to get you back to the woods to demorph."

A *movie*. Movies are an important part of human culture. I had decided, if I was stuck on

11

Earth among these aliens, that I should at least learn about them. Maybe I would never be the big hero Elfangor was, but I could surely become the biggest expert on humans.

Of course, I would have to attend the movie in a morph. I couldn't go around in public in my own Andalite form. Humans would have been terrified. And the Controllers — those humans who are infested by the Yeerk parasites — would have tried to kill me.

Which would have ruined the entire movie experience.

I would have to morph. To take on a different body. But this particular morph was one I had done several times before. I didn't expect there to be any problems.

We were standing together under the camouflage of the forest where I now live. Prince Jake, Marco, Cassie, Rachel, and Tobias were all there. Although Tobias was some distance away.

"Okay, let's do this," Jake said, making sounds with his mouth to form words. He glanced at his watch. "Rachel? You have the backup plan ready? Where does Ax go if he needs an emergency demorph?"

"The dressing rooms at Nordstrom's. They're big and private. Best dressing rooms in the mall. Cassie and I will be posted outside the theater, ready to rush him there if an emergency situation develops."

"And Rachel promises not to stop and shop in Junior Miss on the way," Cassie said, grinning.

Jake glanced up to the sky. Up above the tree-tops, a red-tailed hawk floated on a warm breeze. "Tobias!" Jake yelled.

<All clear,> Tobias called down in thought-speak. <I don't see anyone.>

Tobias is a *nothlit*: a person trapped in a morph. It is what happens if you stay beyond the two-hour limit. Tobias is a human, but his body is that of a hawk. He has adjusted well to this bizarre new life. He lives in the forest with me.

For a long time I expected Tobias to ask me the question that must have haunted him day and night: whether it would ever be possible for him to escape his hawk body. But he never did. I guess he was afraid of the answer. So, I didn't volunteer one.

"Okay," Jake said. "Let's do it."

I began to morph. The first thing I felt was a slipping, melting, almost sickening feeling as my internal organs began to shift around. There was a scary little jolt as my second and third hearts stopped beating. I heard a grinding sound from inside my body as my spine began to shorten.

Soon I was in danger of falling on my face as

13

my front legs shriveled. My arms grew thicker and stronger, but two fingers on each hand melted together to leave me with five-fingered hands.

My shoulders grew wider to support my large arms. And my hind legs grew sturdier as more of my weight was shifted onto them.

The stalks on my head began to retract, and as they did, my stalk eyes grew dimmer and dimmer, like someone turning off the light. Suddenly, they were gone and I only had two eyes.

I dislike that. Having just two eyes is so limiting. You can only look in one direction at a time. You can't even look behind you.

My spine continued to shorten. In fact, it sucked completely out of my tail, which left my tail as limp as a rope. Then the weak remnants of my tail simply withered away.

"Grab him, he's going to fall over," Prince Jake said.

He and Marco each took hold of me to keep me upright, as my front legs disappeared altogether.

"Hey, hey, clothing!" Rachel said, making a face. "Clothing. Don't forget the morphing suit, Ax."

As my body continued to change, my skintight morphing suit also appeared. It is a very difficult trick to be able to morph clothing. And all you can manage is something extremely tight.

"Are you done?" Prince Jake asked me.

I considered. I was standing precariously on two legs. I possessed two strong arms and ten strong fingers. I was mostly without fur. My eyes were weak and totally unable to see anything except what was in front of me. My hearing was good. My mind was functioning normally.

And I had a mouth.

"Yes," I said, using my mouth. "Yessss. Ssssss. Yes-suh. I am in human morph."

I had morphed into a human. The DNA came from samples I had long since acquired from Jake, Cassie, Rachel, and Marco. I would have liked to have Tobias's DNA, but that was not possible since he is a *nothlit*.

My human friends have some differences, but each has only two legs, two arms, and two eyes. They each have one mouth.

Prince Jake is large and pale in color with brown hair. Cassie is shorter and darker in color, with darker brown hair. Marco is also shorter and medium color, with long brown hair. Rachel is taller and pale and has yellow hair.

None of them has any sort of tail.

"This always makes my skin crawl," Marco said, staring at me in a sideways fashion. "It's

15

like the four of us were run through a blender. I swear he has my eyes."

"What's gross is I'll look at him and think, 'Wow, is that guy cute,'" Rachel said. "Then I'll see something that looks like Cassie. Or worse, like *me*!"

"What? Rachel in love with her own looks?" Marco said, using an inflection of his mouth-sounds that humans call sarcasm. Then he looked troubled. "I'm still not sure this is a good idea. The Controllers could —"

"Uh-uh," Prince Jake interrupted. "We're not talking about Controllers, Yeerks, or Visser Three. We are taking a break. We've fought one battle after another. We destroyed the Kandrona. We beat that *Veleek* monster of theirs. And now we are taking some well-deserved vacation time. Ax wants to learn more about humans, so that's what we're doing."

I was never exactly a great student, but I could just imagine how my fellow Andalites would act when they finally rescued me. They'd ask, <So, Aximili, what did you learn about Earth?> And I'd have to say, <Um, well, not much.>

The trick would be to learn about the humans without letting them learn too much about Andalites. There were things I could never tell the humans. Things that might make them turn against me.

"We should hit the Yeerks again while they're weak," Rachel growled. "We know the Yeerks won't get a new ground-based Kandrona for another week. They must still be starving for lack of Kandrona rays. We should hit them!"

Yeerks are a race of parasitic slugs. They live inside the brains of other species. They completely dominate the host body, making it a "Controller." There are Hork-Bajir-Controllers, Taxxon-Controllers, and more and more human-Controllers. Any human you know might be a Controller. There is no way to tell — unless you are an Andalite.

I sympathized with Rachel. But I also understood Prince Jake's caution. No warrior can fight all the time.

"Look, you guys," Prince Jake said. "We hurt the Yeerks. It was a good job. But we also know that they have a replacement Kandrona being set up, so don't assume they're weak. Besides, if they are weak, they sure haven't shown it. I expected to see Yeerks dying left and right, and former Controllers walking free again. Hasn't happened. Somehow they've maintained."

"We can't know what is going on with the Yeerks," Cassie pointed out. "Just because we haven't *seen* them suffer doesn't mean they haven't."

"Okay, look, here we are again, talking about

17

Yeerks," Jake said impatiently. "We have just come from a very, very unpleasant battle. And we came very close to ending up dead. And it's not the first time. So we are *going* to relax and be normal. We are *going* to the movie. And we are *going* to have fun. And no one . . . *Rachel* . . . is going to look for a fight."

"Don't you love it when he gets all forceful like that?" Marco said to Cassie. "He's just so Schwarzenegger sometimes."

"Okay, Ax," Jake said. "Time to get dressed."

"Prince Jake, I am already wearing this garment," I said, pointing to the thing that covered my body. "Wearing. Ing. Ing-uh."

It is an amazing sensation, making sounds with your mouth. Actual words are formed by vibrating your throat and positioning your tongue. But some sounds are better than others. "Ing" is a wonderful sound to make.

"Don't call me 'Prince,'" Prince Jake said.

"Ax, you're dressed like an escapee from the Ice Capades," Marco said.

"You can't go out in public wearing tights and a spandex top," Rachel said. "It's a major fashion 'don't.' Here."

She handed me a bag. In the bag were items of clothing. It took several minutes for me to dress successfully. There is a lot to remember, and every bit of clothing can only go on one way. Socks go on the feet and not on the hands, for example.

When I was done, they all stared at me. Even Tobias flew down to stare.

"Rachel, he looks like he's going to the country club to play polo," Marco said. "I knew we shouldn't let you pick the clothes. He's like a bully magnet. Even I want to beat him up."

"It's a classic look," Rachel said angrily. "Like *you're* Mister Fashion? A person who dresses like Beavis?"

"I think he looks cute," Cassie said.

<Well, that's the kiss of death,> Tobias remarked from his perch in the tree above.

"It is?" I asked.

<Just an expression, Ax-man,> Tobias said. <You'll have fun.>

Ax-man. That's what Tobias calls me sometimes.

"Come on, Ax," Prince Jake said, smiling. "Let's do this. If anyone tries to beat you up, we'll protect you."

CHAPTER 2

"I did not understand the plot of that story," I said.

We were in the movie theater. I was "sitting." This involves bending your body and resting on the fat deposits halfway down the back of your body.

"That was a *preview*, Ax," Prince Jake said. "It's just to give you an idea what the whole movie will be like when it comes out."

"Yes. I see. Why is the screen flat and two-dimensional? Flat. Flat-tuh."

"Because that's how movies are."

"Ah."

"You want some popcorn?" Marco asked. He

held one of the open boxes they had obtained. He moved it close to me.

"Is it food?" I asked.

"Well, sort of," Prince Jake said. "But, Ax? You know how you get around food, okay? So remember — don't get carried away."

I watched Marco eat some of the popcorn. I did as he did. I stuck my large human fingers into the box. I removed a handful of the food and stuck it in my mouth.

I chewed.

The texture was rough and strange. And the flavor! It reminded me of a food called pizza. But there was just a hint of cigarette butts, which I also enjoy. Although Prince Jake had told me never to eat cigarette butts again. They are bad for you.

I took another handful of the popcorn. I chewed it. Another handful.

"This is excellent!" I cried.

"It tastes like it's about a week old," Marco said.

"What are these flavors? What are they called?"

"I don't know. Salt? Grease?"

"Salt!" I said, savoring the very sound of the word. "Salt! And grease! Greee-suh!"

"Hey, hold it down," someone behind me said. "The movie is starting."

21

"Salt. Salt-tuh. Grease. Greeeesss."

"Ax, don't talk so loud, okay?" Prince Jake suggested.

"Here, just take the box," Marco said.

He handed me the box of popcorn. I quickly ate the rest of it.

"Not the *box*!" Marco wailed. "You don't eat the *box*!"

"It tasted of salt and grease," I pointed out.

"Oh, man. Is it time to leave yet?" Marco asked Prince Jake. "Tell me it's time to leave."

The movie began. It involved humans and nonhumans in uniforms. It seemed they were in some sort of spacecraft.

"What type of ship is that?" I asked. "It looks somewhat like a Hawjabran freighter."

"That's the *Enterprise*," Prince Jake said. "It's not real. It's just made-up."

"Yes, I know," I said. "I *do* know what a real interstellar spacecraft looks like."

Marco and Prince Jake looked at each other. Both smiled.

I quickly became bored by the plot of the movie. For one thing, there was one character who was clearly an Ongachic female. But in the movie this creature was called a "Klingon." It made no sense.

However, by accident I made a tremendous

discovery: There was *more* popcorn! It was in boxes on the floor. I hadn't seen it in the darkness. There was a half-full box right by my feet.

I quickly ate this new popcorn. Then I found something else beside it on the floor. It was a smaller box. Inside it were three small, brown globules.

I ate the brown globules.

At that moment, it was as if the entire planet had stopped spinning. The taste! It was beyond description!

Those brown globules were like nothing I had ever experienced. I felt my life had changed. I felt myself lifted up out of the world of everyday senses to some new level.

More! I wanted more!

I dropped to my knees and began to search. I crawled along the floor, looking for more. It was easier crawling than walking. At least when I crawled I had four legs. Also, the humans had coated the floor with sticky substances, which made it easier not to slip.

I found no more boxes of globules. However, there was a small, twisted plastic envelope. And within that twisted plastic envelope I discovered a chunk that smelled very similar to the globules.

I stuck it in my mouth.

Yes! It was the same flavor. The same miraculous, heavenly flavor! And yet . . . there were differences, too. It was crunchier. And there were other flavors.

The floor of the movie theater was filled with precious items! I crawled on. I had to squeeze past several seated humans who made loud noises as I passed.

"Hey, jerk! What are you doing?"

"Get away from me, you freak!"

But I could not be distracted. I wanted more of the amazing brown food! More!

Yes! Success! Another small box, and this one was half filled with brightly colored pellets. And yet, inside each pellet, more of the magic brown food!

More. More! I wanted more!

There! A younger human was holding an entire box of the brown globules! But I could not just take them. I must have permission first.

I looked up from the floor at the human. "Please give me your brown globules?!" I asked. "Globules! Ules!"

"MOMMY!"

"What do you think you're doing?" another human cried.

"MOMMY! He's trying to take my candy!"

I heard a more familiar voice. It was Marco. "Where is he? Jake! Where's Ax?"

"I merely wish to enjoy the brown globules!" I explained to the screaming child.

Suddenly, I felt Prince Jake and Marco grabbing my arms. They lifted me up off the floor and dragged me away.

"Globules!" I cried. I snatched for the box the small human was holding. "Globules!"

CHAPTER 3

There are many dangers for an Andalite in human morph. For one thing, there is the constant danger that you will fall off your two legs. The slightest push and you can topple over. But worse by far is the danger of taste. Taste is the sense that can drive an Andalite mad! Especially if it involves cinnamon buns or chocolate.
— **From the Earth Diary of Aximili-Esgarrouth-Isthill**

By the time Marco and Prince Jake had half-dragged, half-carried me out of the theater, I was calm again. We emerged into a brilliant sunlit area where vehicles are parked.

"Okay, I think we have learned a lesson here," Prince Jake said. "No chocolate for Ax."

"Chocolate? Chock? Chock-lit?" I said, trying out the word. "The brown globules are called chocolate? What about the brightly colored pellets?"

"Actually, the globules are called Raisinets.

The pellets are M&M's. Are you under control now, Ax?" Prince Jake asked.

I couldn't tell if he was angry or amused. "Yes," I said shakily. "I . . . the flavor! It was just so wonderful."

Cassie and Rachel emerged from the mall behind me. They watched curiously, but kept their distance. As always, we were careful not to appear to be a group. The Controllers are everywhere.

Suddenly, I heard a thought-speak message. <Hey, you guys. Was the movie that bad?>

It was Tobias, on patrol far overhead. Of course, no one could answer him. Humans can use thought-speech only when they're in a morph. And since I was in a human body, I too was restricted to spoken language.

<There's kind of a thing going on,> Tobias said. <Just around the corner from you. Some guy staggering around and screaming at the top of his lungs. Cops are coming fast. I'm pretty sure I heard the word 'Yeerk.' He's heading your way.>

Just then, I began to hear it, too. It was a human shouting in a loud, hoarse voice.

"Over there," Marco said tersely.

A man appeared. He seemed to be having difficulty standing up. He leaned against the outer wall of the store and staggered forward. Humans stared at him and moved away.

27

"Listen to me! Listen to me!" he cried, looking around wildly. "They're here! They're here! They're everywhere! The Yeerks are here!"

My human body felt as if it had been jolted with electricity. Human bodies become very tense when surprised. I could see that Prince Jake and Marco were having the same reaction.

I heard sirens wailing and drawing closer.

"What do we do?" Marco asked.

Prince Jake turned quickly back to Rachel and Cassie. He made a gesture with his hand. "Split up!" he said.

"They're heeeeere!" the man cried. "Aaaaah-hhh!" He suddenly clapped both his hands over his left ear. "Got you! Got you! Die! Die!"

"He's a Controller," I said. "The Yeerk in his head is dying."

Jake met my gaze. "I know," he said. "Been there."

I nodded. Jake had been made into a Controller, though only for a brief time. We had been able to imprison him and starve the Yeerk. Yeerks live in the brains of other species, but every three Earth days they must bathe in the Yeerk pool and soak up Kandrona rays. Without Kandrona rays, they starve and die.

Kandrona rays are beamed from a device called a Kandrona. (Actually, it's a Kandrona Wave/Particle Generator.) The rays are beamed and then concentrated in the Yeerk pool, where the Yeerks feed.

We had found and destroyed the Earth-based Kandrona.

"Why is this happening *now?*" Rachel asked. "It's been weeks since we destroyed the Kandrona. Nothing ever seemed to happen. So why now?"

I shrugged my shoulders, the way humans do to indicate ignorance. "I don't know, Rachel. Maybe the Yeerks have reached their limit. It would have been a strain on their resources to shuttle Controllers back and forth to the mother ship. Ship-puh. Maybe something was broken."

"I didn't think things just broke for you space people," Marco said.

"Things break," I said truthfully. "Break. Ake. Ake-kuh."

"Well, whatever. Scratch one Yeerk," Marco said harshly.

The man was screaming now and yanking at his ear. I could just see the slimy tip of the dying Yeerk as it slithered out of the man's head.

"Can't we help him?"

It was Cassie. She and Rachel had defied Prince Jake's order to split up. They were with us now as we watched, horrified and transfixed.

"We have to stay clear of this," Prince Jake said. "But maybe it's finally starting. It may just

29

be this one guy, but there may be more. Finally! I expected this to start happening weeks ago. Yeerks dying! Controllers suddenly free and human again." He grinned. It was a savage look. "They'll die, and their hosts will be free! At first, people will think they're nuts. But when they have ten, twenty, fifty people all yelling about the Yeerks? They won't be able to cover that up. Not for long!"

His voice had risen, becoming higher, and the words came out faster. He was obviously excited.

Suddenly, an ambulance raced up, followed by two police cars, all with flashing lights and screaming sirens.

"Hah!" Marco said. "I'm sure some of the cops are Controllers, but they can't all be. Jake's right. The truth will get out! This is going to work! The truth is going to come out!"

"The replacement Kandrona is supposed to be here soon," Rachel pointed out. "We should have seen a lot more of this. The Yeerks must have found a way to keep this from happening till now."

Rachel is a true warrior. She does not underestimate her enemies. She was not ready to start talking about victory.

But the others were all very happy. They believed that many Yeerks would die, and the hosts would be free to tell the world the truth.

They believed they had won the war.

It made me sad for them. Because I knew the truth. I knew how the Yeerks operated.

I almost told Prince Jake right then. He has a special reason to be hopeful. His brother, Tom, is a Controller. There is nothing Prince Jake would want as much as his brother's freedom.

But I knew this screaming Controller with the dying Yeerk in his head was just an oversight. Something had gone wrong with the Yeerk's secret efforts, but I knew that there would be no witnesses.

I knew what would happen to this poor, shouting human.

Jake was my prince now, my leader. But if I told him . . . it would lead to questions. And I could not answer questions. Not without revealing the terrible truth behind the law of *Seerow's Kindness.*

Humans rushed from the ambulance and the police cars. Most, as Marco had said, were probably true, normal humans. They grabbed the screaming man, who was still pulling the Yeerk from his ear.

"Oh, Lord! What is that? He's pulling his brains out!" one policeman cried in horror.

"The Yeerks! They're here!" the human screamed. "Die! Die! Get out of me and die! Freedom!"

31

The police surrounded the man and hustled him to the ambulance. It was hard to see, unless you were expecting it: the moment when one of the policemen drew a small, steel cylinder from his pocket and pressed it against the back of the man's neck.

"I can't believe it!" Cassie exulted. "Maybe it's really going to happen. Maybe people will realize the truth!"

"They have a real, live Yeerk now," Prince Jake said. "They can't cover this up forever."

Again I thought of telling them the truth. That the human was already gone. That the Yeerk slug would crumble into dust. That no evidence would be left behind.

But even though these humans were my friends, even though we fought side by side, there were secrets I could not tell them.

I could not tell them how a race of parasitic slugs had come to be a danger to the entire galaxy.

I could not tell them why we Andalites had to fight the Yeerks. Why we had no choice but to fight them. Why we hated them so deeply.

We have secrets, we Andalites. And the greatest secret of all is our own guilt.

"This is great," Prince Jake said, smiling.

"Yes," I said. "Great."

CHAPTER 4

$\prod$s the sun rose above the horizon the next morning, I stood by the small stream where I drink each day. Rough grasses, mixed with fallen leaves and pine needles, ran right down to the water. The sun was just barely visible through a gap in the forest trees.

<From the water that gave birth to us,> I said, and dipped my right forehoof into the water. It was the beginning of the morning ritual.

<From the grass that feeds us,> I said, and moved back to crush a small tuft of grass beneath the same hoof.

<For the freedom that unites us.> I spread my arms wide.

33

<We rise to the stars.> I looked with all four of my eyes at the rising sun.

I sighed. This was really pretty pointless. I had never been a big believer in all the rituals. I mean, if you're going to be a warrior, you have to do it. And any *aristh* who gets caught rushing through the ritual is verbally reprimanded.

But still, I was about a billion Earth miles from my home world. It was hard to see why I should still be acting like a good little warrior-cadet. I was all alone among aliens. Who cared if I performed the rituals?

I bowed low. <Freedom is my only cause. Duty to the people, my only guide. Obedience to my prince, my only glory.>

I hesitated. Tobias had landed in the tree above.

<The destruction of my enemies, my most solemn vow.>

I straightened up again, then assumed the fighting stance. <I, Aximili-Esgarrouth-Isthill, Andalite warrior-cadet, offer my life.>

With that, I drew my tail blade forward and pressed it against my own throat.

Then I relaxed my tail. This was the part of the ritual that called for contemplation. You were supposed to think about the parts of the ritual and ask yourself if you were living up to all of it.

The destruction of my enemies, my most

solemn vow. That was the part that stayed in my thoughts.

I had not destroyed my enemy. My enemy was terrible and powerful. And if I tried to destroy him, I would be the one killed.

But that did not matter. What mattered was the enemy. The creature who had murdered my brother. Not in battle, but as he lay almost helpless.

It was the humans who'd told me the rest of Elfangor's story. As the dome went crashing into Earth's sea, my brother's fighter was damaged by the Yeerks.

He landed in an abandoned construction site. There were five human youths passing by: Jake, Cassie, Marco, Rachel, and Tobias.

Elfangor was dying, and he knew that Earth was now defenseless. He told the five youths about the Yeerk threat. And then he did what he should not have done. He gave them a weapon to fight the Yeerks.

He gave them the Andalite power to morph.

Never in all of history has any non-Andalite been given the power to morph. It's against our major law: the law of *Seerow's Kindness*.

Only one other creature can morph: the Yeerk who invaded and took over an Andalite body. He is the only Andalite-Controller. There are hundreds of thousands of Hork-Bajir and Taxxons

35

and humans enslaved that way, but only one Andalite.

Only one Yeerk has an Andalite body, and the power to morph.

The Abomination: Visser Three.

The humans told me of Elfangor's last battle. How Visser Three had morphed into a huge, monstrous creature. How Elfangor had fought to the very end, lashing out helplessly. How Visser Three had opened his jaws and . . .

The humans don't know it, but if Elfangor had lived, he would have been in huge trouble. He would have been demoted, at very least. He would no longer have been a prince. Elfangor as the great hero would have been finished.

<The destruction of my enemies, my most solemn vow.>

I had faced Visser Three more than once. He was still living. I had no excuse, except that I was still just an *aristh*. If I were a full warrior, it would have been total dishonor for me.

Elfangor would have had the courage. If it had been me killed by Visser Three, Elfangor would have gone right after him.

But I guess I'm not Elfangor.

<Hey, Ax-man, what's up?>

<I am fine, Tobias,> I said. Actually, I was not fine. Tobias being there reminded me that I had something planned for this morning, and I was

nervous. Maybe that's why the morning ritual had not left me feeling calm, like it was supposed to. I was planning to do something very frightening. I was planning to go to school.

<Not to be too curious or anything, but what was that you were doing? I've seen you do it before.>

<The morning ritual. It reminds a warrior to be humble. And to serve the people.>

<Sounds good,> Tobias said. <Yikes! Um, Ax? Don't step back. In fact, don't move at all.>

<What is wrong?> I asked.

<Don't you hear that?>

I listened. <That rattling, hissing sound? I've heard that before.>

<It's a rattlesnake. Right by your leg. They're poisonous, you know.>

<Ah. No, I didn't know.> I turned to face the snake. I saw it coiled in the leaves. What I did not see was when it struck! It was too fast! Too fast to see, let alone avoid.

Luckily, the fangs hit my hoof! I whipped my tail forward and pressed the snake against the ground, holding it immobile. It squirmed and made the rattling sound with its tail.

<Better get rid of it,> Tobias advised.

But I had a different idea. I focused on the snake. I began to "acquire" it, absorbing the snake's DNA into my system.

37

<You want to be able to morph a rattlesnake?> Tobias asked, sounding dubious.

<It's very fast,> I said. <And I have fewer Earth morphs than the others. It may be useful someday.> The snake had gone limp, the way animals always do when you acquire them. When I was done and the snake's DNA was within me, I used my tail to flip it away into some bushes.

<So,> Tobias asked, <are you still going ahead with your get-to-know-the-humans plan?>

<Yes. I may be on this planet for a long time. I should be using this time to learn about humans. Even though . . . I think I may have behaved badly at the movie.>

Tobias laughed. He laughed for quite a while. <Yeah. I heard about that. You just need to stay away from chocolate.>

<I am not prepared for taste. The experience is very powerful. Perhaps I should not morph into a human anymore.>

<Don't sweat it,> Tobias said. <But speaking of taste . . . you realize there's this big mystery about you.>

<A big mystery?>

<Yeah. No one wants to ask you because they think maybe it's rude. But everyone wants to know how you eat with no mouth.>

<How I eat?> I repeated, puzzled. <Well, I have hooves, don't I?>

<Ooookay,> Tobias said. <I'll mind my own business.>

We started moving through the woods. I ran at a good speed. I enjoyed leaping fallen logs and dodging through dense patches of thorny bushes. I was getting to know this forest well.

As I ran and leaped, Tobias flew overhead. At times he would rise through the canopy of trees and disappear from my sight. At other times he would flit from tree to tree, silent, swift.

<In school, during Xenobiology, we had a section on humans,> I told Tobias. <It mostly involved human television programs. News shows. Entertainment. Music.>

<Music? You mean like MTV? You were watching music videos on the Andalite home world?>

<I don't remember what they were. I . . . I didn't pay very much attention to Xenobiology. I wish I had now. A warrior is supposed to be a scientist and an artist, as well as a fighter. But I didn't always enjoy that other stuff, so I didn't pay much attention. I suppose humans always pay attention in school.>

<Absolutely,> Tobias said. <That's why I am such an expert on the War of 1812.>

<A war? Tell me about it.>

<I was kidding. I don't know anything about the War of 1812. We're just about there. Are you ready to start?>

39

We had reached a narrow spur of woods. Normally, I would not have dared go this far because it was surrounded on three sides by human habitations. But Tobias was overhead, keeping his incredibly keen eyes open for any danger.

<Yes, I'm ready.>

<Jake and Cassie are coming across the field. Time for you to morph. Time to get human.>

<Tobias, will you . . . I mean, you'll be alone today. While I'm with the others.>

<What, like I can't get along without you, Axman? I have places to go. Things to do. Feathers to preen. Rodents to eat. Besides, Ax, Jake has already asked me to fly cover over the school while you're in there.>

I don't know why, but it made me feel better to think that Tobias would be in the sky above me all day.

Sometimes I think Tobias and I could be true *shorm*. A *shorm* is a deep friend, someone you never lie to, someone who knows all your secrets. The word *shorm* means "tail blade." See, it's supposed to mean a person you would trust so much they could put their tail blade right up against your throat and you wouldn't even worry.

Sometimes I think Tobias and I could be like that. We are both cut off from our own people. We're both alone.

But if we were friends, I would have no secrets from Tobias. And even though he was a hawk in form, he was still a human. And I am an Andalite. And no matter how much I sometimes wished for a real friend, there had to be a wall between my people and the humans. Between me and the humans.

Getting too close to any alien species is a mistake. We are taught that. We may protect them, defend them, care for them. But they can never be deep friends.

CHAPTER 5

I have morphed some Andalite animals. And I have
morphed many strange Earth animals. But the animal
I morphed the most is the human animal. They are
weak, slow, half-blind, and unstable, but no Andalite
should laugh at them. Humans rule their planet. And
as the human Rachel once said, Earth is a tough
neighborhood.
  — **From the Earth Diary of Aximili-Esgarrouth-Isthill**

I peered through the trees. I could see a
wide, grassy field. On the far side of the field
were several long, squat buildings. There were
large yellow vehicles parked in front. Hundreds
of young humans milled around outside the
building.

Prince Jake and Cassie had drawn close.

"Hey, Ax," Prince Jake said. "How's it going?"

<Very well, Prince Jake,> I answered.

"Um, you're not going to call me *Prince* Jake
today, are you?"

<When I am in human morph, I will behave as a normal human,> I assured him.

"Well, better go ahead and morph," Cassie suggested.

<I think we're clear, but I'll go up and take a look,> Tobias said. He flapped his wings and rose slowly into the sky.

I concentrated on my human morph and began to make the change.

<Still clear,> I heard Tobias call down from above. <There are some kids about two hundred feet away, but they can't see you.>

I morphed as quickly as I could, while being careful not to fall over as my third and fourth legs disappeared. At last, I stood on just two legs. It's both frightening and exciting. I mean, there you are, tottering back and forth with nothing to hold you up. Your feet can't grip, and they are too short to be much help in balancing.

All you can do if you start to fall is stand on one leg while you throw the second leg out to catch yourself. It's very unreliable. I don't know why humans evolved this way. They are the only species on this planet to walk around on just two legs, without wings or a tail to hold them up.

And I've certainly never heard of any other intelligent species trying to walk this way.

"Hey, grab him," Prince Jake yelled as I began to lean back.

"Got him," Cassie said. She helped support me as I finished the morph.

Last of all the mouth appeared, a horizontal split in my face.

"Are you done?" Prince Jake asked me.

"Yes. I am fully human." The sound delighted me. It's an amazing talent, this ability to make complex sounds. "Human. Mun. Hyew-mun. Human. Huh-yew-mun."

"Um, Ax? Don't do that, okay?" Prince Jake said.

"What? What-tuh?"

"That. Where you play with every sound like it's a new toy."

"Yes, my prince. Not a toy. Toy! Toytoytoytoy . . . Sorry."

"This should be interesting," Cassie said, looking at Prince Jake.

Tobias came swooping low and rested on a tree branch. <It's kind of sweet,> he said. <Ax's first day of school.>

"His *only* day of school," Prince Jake said quickly. "This is just so he can learn how to be a more believable human. One time."

Prince Jake held up a single finger, indicating the number one.

"Yes, that is one," I agreed. "Now, let's go to school. I am looking forward to it. To it. Tewit."

"Remember, you're my cousin Phillip, from out of state," Jake said while handing me a bag filled with garments.

"Phillip," I repeated confidently. "Phillip. Lip. Phill-up. Pah."

I like the sound the letter "p" makes.

I got dressed and set off toward the squat building that was the schoolhouse.

<Have fun,> Tobias said. He sounded just a little wistful in my mind. It was a strange thing, I guess. I, an alien, could go to his school. But he could not.

"I will," I called back over my shoulder.

Unfortunately, bending that way made me fall over. It takes practice to walk on just two legs.

CHAPTER 6

"Here it is," Cassie said. "School. Or, as I like to think of it — purgatory."

The school was very active. There were large numbers of humans racing about at high speed. Others moved very slowly and seemed sad or ill. Many carried books. Most made mouth-sounds.

As usual they were dressed in a shocking variety of clothing. Clothing is not a uniquely human idea, but of course Andalites do not indulge in it.

However, when I am in human morph I must wear clothing. All of my human friends, even Tobias, agree on this. They agree very strongly on this one point.

I saw Rachel and Marco approaching through the crowd of humans.

My other human friends tell me that Rachel is beautiful and Marco is cute. As an Andalite, I don't observe either trait. However, when I am in human morph I begin to see that Rachel actually is very beautiful.

But I never see that Marco is cute.

At school, the Animorphs must pretend not to be very close. This is so any suspicious human-Controllers will not begin to think of them as a "group."

"Hi, Marco, Rachel," Prince Jake said. "Meet my cousin . . . Phillip."

"Yes. I am Prince Jake's cousin, Phillip," I said. "I am from out of state."

Marco made a smile with his mouth. "You're from way, way out of state."

"Don't call me 'Prince,'" Prince Jake hissed.

"Nice to see you again, Phillip," Rachel said and winked. Since she was *really* Jake's cousin, she would have already met "Phillip." "See you guys later. Good luck."

"You'll need it," Marco added.

We went inside the school building. It seemed to be nothing but a very long corridor. It was filled with humans. Along each side of the corridor there were doors. Some of the doors were large. But there were hundreds of much

47

smaller doors. I observed people opening the small doors, but no one ever went inside.

"Where do the small doors lead?" I asked.

"Nowhere. Those are lockers," Cassie said. "Everyone has a locker. See? There's my locker right there."

We went to Cassie's locker. It was decorated with a shiny pendant. The pendant had a wheel with numbers on it. Cassie spun the wheel back and forth.

"Is that a ritual?" I asked. "Chew-ull. Ritual."

"No, that's a lock. It keeps people out."

"Why?"

"So they won't steal my stuff." She opened her locker and began putting things in and taking things out.

"What is that?" I asked. "Thuh-at. That."

"It's just a picture," Cassie said. She quickly closed the door of her locker.

"It looked like a picture of Prin . . . of Jake," I pointed out. "Why would you have a picture of him when he is right here and you can see him?"

Cassie shrugged and looked down at the ground. Humans have many facial expressions. I believe this one indicated either sickness or em-barrassment.

"Come on, Ax," Prince Jake said. He was

smiling at Cassie and she was continuing to look sick or embarrassed. "We'll see you later, Cassie. Time for first —"

Just then, a terrible, mind-shattering sound! BBBBBRRRRRRRIIIIINNNNNGGGG!

I spun around. I raised my human arms, ready to use them for defense. I wished I had my tail. It's a terrible thing to be without a tail in a fight. But I was ready to do the best I could with my human body.

"Ax! I mean, Phillip. Relax."

BBBBBBBBRRRRRRIIIIIIINNNNNGGGG!

"That noise!" I cried. "What kind of beast is it?"

"Ax, it's just the bell for first period," Jake said. "Take it easy. People are staring."

"It's not a threat?"

"No. It's not a threat. It's depressing, but not dangerous."

I followed Prince Jake as he led the way down the hall. It was difficult to forget the horrible noise. When humans are threatened their bodies are flooded with a chemical that make them hyper-alert, fearful, and aggressive. The chemical is called adrenalin. My system was now flooded with adrenalin. It was very distracting.

We entered one of the large doors. Inside were approximately thirty humans arranged in small, confining seats. At the front of the room was a large table. An older human stood there.

"Everyone get to your seats," the older human said.

Prince Jake said, "Mr. Pardue? This is my cousin from out of town. His name's Phillip. He's just hanging with me today, okay?"

"Just sit. Sit. Be quiet and sit."

I could tell from Prince Jake's facial expression that he was troubled. He took my arm and led me to the back of the room.

"Take that desk," Prince Jake said.

"Take it where? Wheh-err? Where?"

"I mean sit in it."

I understood sitting. I was getting pretty good at passing for human.

Once, for two days I had to morph Prince Jake and pretend to be him. I was successful in fooling his parents and brother. Although I later learned that his parents believed "he" had become mentally ill. When the real Prince Jake returned, they took him to see a doctor.

"Sitting in this desk is unpleasant," I said.

"You got that right, dude," a human I didn't know said.

"What is going on back there? Quiet down," the teacher demanded loudly. "What is . . . what . . . wha . . ." Suddenly, he clutched at his head with both hands. "Everyone be quiet! Quiet!"

Now Prince Jake looked very troubled. "Mr. Pardue, are you okay?"

All the other humans stared at the teacher, too. Everyone was very quiet.

"Okay?" Mr. Pardue demanded in a loud, angry voice. "Am I okay? Am I — aaaaahhhhh!"

Without warning, Mr. Pardue pitched forward. He fell on the floor. He clawed at his head with his hands.

And he cried. "Yeerk! Get out of me!"

He clawed at his head till blood began to flow.

CHAPTER 7

"Aaaaaarrrggghhh!" the teacher cried as he clawed at his head.

One of the humans began screaming. "What's happening?! What's happening?!"

Someone else ran from the room into the hallway and began to shout, "Help! Help! Help!"

Prince Jake and I sat very still, side by side in the back of the room.

"Stop damaging our body!" Mr. Pardue cried. Then, as if he were answering himself, he said in a slurred voice, "Get out my head! Get out of my head! You're finished!"

Prince Jake's gaze met my own. We both knew what was happening.

"That makes two," Prince Jake whispered.

"Two that we've seen. Something is going wrong for . . . for them."

Mr. Pardue began crying. He began cursing. All the while he writhed on the floor, and the other humans stood around horrified, helpless.

"Did you know this teacher was a Controller?" I asked Prince Jake, making my voice very quiet.

"No. He always seemed like a nice guy. I can't just sit here and watch this!"

"Get OUT OF ME!" Mr. Pardue screamed suddenly.

The Yeerk in the teacher's head was weakening. It was starving from lack of Kandrona rays. The human host, the real Mr. Pardue, was fighting for control.

Suddenly, Prince Jake stood up and rushed to the teacher's side. I was right behind him. I tried to grab his arm to stop him, but he was too quick.

"Prince Jake!" I snapped, but he ignored me.

Prince Jake knelt by the teacher's bleeding head. "I know what this is," he whispered. "I know what this is, Mr. Pardue. Ride it out. The Yeerk will die. You'll be free."

Others were coming closer. Close enough to overhear. "Stay back," I said to them. "There may be danger."

I didn't know what else to say. It seemed to work. The others stayed back.

Mr. Pardue rolled his eyes up to focus blearily on Prince Jake's face.

Prince Jake grabbed the teacher's shoulder in a tight grip. "I've been there," he whispered. "I've done it, Mr. Pardue. I was a Controller for a while. I survived. Just hang in."

I searched the faces of the other humans, trying to see if they had overheard. Jake was my prince, but this was dangerous, foolish behavior.

Suddenly, the door of the room opened. I recognized the human who rushed into the room.

Chapman.

He is the assistant principal for the school. He is also a high-ranking Controller.

"All right, kids, everyone out," Chapman snapped. "Everyone out to the playground. Out of the building. Mr. Pardue is just sick."

"You!" Mr. Pardue cried. "No! Chapman is . . . he's . . ."

"I said OUT!" Chapman roared.

The humans fled the room, anxious to be away from the scene of madness.

But Prince Jake did not move. He stayed by the human called Pardue. I saw his fists clenching. There was a dangerous light in his eyes.

Chapman looked at me. Then back at Prince Jake. "Jake, you and your friend get out."

For a frozen moment of time, no one moved. I held my breath. Would Prince Jake start a fight?

If so, I would have to join him. But this was a foolish fight. Prince Jake could not afford to reveal himself.

I grabbed Prince Jake's arm and yanked him up to his feet. He glared furiously at me.

"We have to go," I said.

Slowly he nodded. "Yeah. Hope he gets better." He looked at Chapman. "He will get better, won't he, Mr. Chapman?"

"Who can say?" the Controller answered coldly.

I drew Prince Jake away. He stopped at the door, and we looked back to see Chapman draw a short steel cylinder from his pocket. He pressed it against the neck of the weeping teacher.

"No!" Mr. Pardue cried. "No!"

Then, very quickly, Mr. Pardue fell silent.

Prince Jake turned away and ran. He pushed his way through the others, who were still clustered just outside the classroom. He ran clear outside. He gasped at the air, as if he did not have sufficient oxygen.

I caught up to him, but it was difficult. He has more practice running on two legs.

"Prince . . . I mean, Jake. Are you sick?"

He shook his head. "Pardue was a Controller. The Yeerk was starving. And why? Because we destroyed the Kandrona. Me and you and the others. We did this!"

"It was necessary," I said. "We struck a powerful blow against the Yeerks by destroying the Kandrona."

"Chapman killed him, didn't he?" Prince Jake said. "The little steel cylinder. Did you see that? Not just the Yeerk, but the real Pardue. He killed them both."

There was no point in lying anymore. Prince Jake had seen the truth. And the idea of lying now, here, made me feel unwell inside.

"If the Yeerk inside the teacher had died, the teacher would have survived and been free," I said. "He would have told other humans what happened. He would have warned them. The Yeerks can't allow witnesses."

"They're going to kill every host whose Yeerk dies, aren't they?" Prince Jake asked bitterly. "Every human-Controller whose Yeerk dies is going to be eliminated. That's true, isn't it?"

"Yes."

Prince Jake's face showed an expression. I believed it was an expression of sickness.

"We did this," Prince Jake said.

"It's war," I said.

"My brother," Prince Jake said. "Tom. He's a Controller. What about him?"

I had no answer. The Yeerks would save as many as they could. But if their emergency system was breaking down, they would do what had to be done. They would eliminate any evidence.

Prince Jake was staring at me. "You *knew* they would do this?"

I glared back at him. Maybe it was the human adrenalin in my system, but I was becoming angry now. Angry at the accusing look in Prince Jake's eyes. "Yes, I knew."

"How did you know?"

I hesitated. Prince Jake did not like my hesitation. He suddenly wheeled around and pushed me against the wall.

"How did you know the Yeerks would do this?"

"Because it's happened before. You think this is the first planet the Yeerks have infiltrated? Do you think Earth is the only place where we Andalites have fought them? They don't leave witnesses."

Prince Jake let me go. But he looked at me with unmistakable suspicion. "I don't like you keeping secrets from me, Ax. I'm your friend. We're your friends. We should know whatever you know. You didn't tell me about this."

"Terrible things happen in war," I said. "You did what you had to do. Destroying the Kandrona was part of that war."

"You can say it's a war," Prince Jake said. "But I hate it."

"Love the warrior. Hate the war. War-ruh."

"What is that, an old Andalite saying?" Prince Jake asked sarcastically.

"Yes. My brother used to say it."

Prince Jake looked at me for a very long time. It made me uncomfortable. "You know something, Ax? Sometimes I get the feeling we humans are just pawns in this big game between you Andalites and the Yeerks. We're just ammunition in this war, aren't we? Too dumb to know what's going on. Too primitive to be real warriors."

"That is not the way it is," I said. My own anger was diminishing. Prince Jake's suspicion was not.

"You fight alongside us, Ax. As far as I'm concerned, you're one of us. But then I find out you're keeping secrets. Rachel and Marco keep asking me: What do we know about Ax? What has he ever told us about his own planet, while we show him everything? I told them we could trust you. Now I wonder. I *really* wonder. There's no trust when you keep secrets. You should have told me this is what the Yeerks would do. You know I have a brother who . . . you know about Tom. I had a right to know what could happen."

"Maybe you would not have destroyed the Kandrona if you had known it could endanger Tom," I pointed out.

Prince Jake stuck his face very close to mine. "That's what you think? You know what, Ax? You're right to try and learn more about humans. Because you don't know a thing about us. Not a thing."

CHAPTER 8

An Andalite may think that humans are simple, open, trusting creatures. But they are more subtle than they seem to be at first. Possibly this is because of their spoken language, where no word ever means just one thing.
— **From the Earth Diary of Aximili-Esgarrouth-Isthill**

My day at the human school ended with the removal of the teacher who had been a Controller. Prince Jake went home. I went back to the woods and gratefully resumed my true shape.

But I spent a very bad afternoon and night. I realized that Prince Jake and the humans could never be true *shorms*. I knew there was a wall between me and them. But they were all I had. Without them, I was utterly alone. And Prince Jake's anger and suspicion had hurt me.

It is a terribly lonely thing to be a billion Earth miles from every living member of your own people.

The next day, Marco invited me to "hang out" with him. This was a surprise. Marco has never been very friendly, unlike Cassie and Tobias and Prince Jake. Rachel, too, has never seemed to take to me.

I morphed into my human body and met Marco at the edge of the woods.

"So," he said. "You want to be Pinocchio, huh?"

"What?"

"Pinocchio was a little boy carved out of wood. He wanted to be a real, live human."

"I do not want to *be* a human. I merely wish to study them."

Marco smiled. "What a coincidence. And I want to study Andalites."

It took several minutes for me to understand what he was saying. "Oh. Prince Jake asked you to press me for information."

"Jake was a little ticked off that you didn't tell us everything you know," Marco said. "Rachel was even more ticked. Come on, we have to catch the bus. You want to learn about humans, right? I thought I'd take you to a bookstore. Smart as you are, you can learn to read English."

"Bookstore? Book-kuh-store?"

"Yeah. Books. Fiction. History. A hundred thousand books all about the human race. And you get to choose any of them you want. We have no secrets, unlike certain species I could mention who don't even tell us a little thing like how they eat with no mouth."

"I see. You open your society to me. Societeee. Teee. And you want me to do the same in return."

"I told Jake I could cleverly weasel all the information out of you, but he said, 'No, Ax is a friend. Show him we have nothing to hide. Maybe he'll finally decide to trust us.'"

I felt a pang of guilt. They were treating me with trust. They had never done anything to hurt me. On the contrary, they had been wonderful to me. Good in every way.

"I have reasons for keeping secrets," I said.

Marco nodded. "Yeah, we know. Rachel says you probably aren't allowed to interfere with primitive races like humans."

I was surprised. It was very close to the truth. At first I did not know what to say.

Marco smiled a cold smile and nodded his head. "So that is it, right? Kind of too late for that attitude, isn't it? After all, the Yeerks are interfering with us like crazy."

I had no answer to give. But as I looked around at the street, at all the humans in their cars, and all the humans lurching along on two legs, it occurred to me just how defenseless I would be without Prince Jake and Marco and the others.

We had reached the bus stop. Suddenly Marco slapped his pants. "Oh, man. I left my money at home. We all pitched in for your book fund. I left it on my desk. Come on."

"Where are we going? Ing? Ing-ahng-ing. That is a *very* satisfying sound."

"Yeah, everybody loves a good 'ing.' We have to run over to my house. Don't worry, it's just around the corner."

Marco led me down the street. There were houses on both sides. Big, boxy structures with transparent rectangles here and there.

"That is Prince Jake's house," I said. I had spent time in Prince Jake's house.

"No, it's just the same model as his house. This is a subdivision. There are only like five different models of houses. They all look alike. Welcome to the suburbs. But it beats the place I used to live in."

He was correct. There were only five types of house. Although some had more grass, and some had less. Also, some houses were decorated with items that had been placed on the grass.

"What is that decoration?" I asked.

Marco followed the direction of my gaze. Then he rolled his eyes upward. "That's a Big Wheel."

"It is very attractive. Very colorful."

"Uh-huh. I'd love to tell you how it works, but it's the very height of human technology, so it's secret. Primitive races could get hold of Big Wheels, and then who knows what might happen?"

I am still learning about human mouth-sounds. But I am very sure Marco's sound was "sarcasm."

"There's my house. My dad is home, working. He sprained his ankle, so he's using his home computer. Don't be weird, okay?"

"No. I will not be weird. Weeeerd. Weeeeer-duh. I will act like a normal human."

"You act like a normal human and you'll win an Oscar," Marco said. He led the way up to his house and opened the door. "Okay, look, you wait right there by that table. Don't go anywhere. If my dad comes in and talks to you, just say 'yes' and 'no.' Got it? Yes and no answers only. I'll run up to my room. I'm gonna call one of the others to meet us at the bookstore. You're already driving me nuts."

I stood by the table. There was a primitive computer on the table. It even had a solid, two-dimensional screen. And a keyboard! An actual keyboard.

I touched the keyboard. It was amazing. Andalite computers once had keyboards, too. Although ours were very different. And it had been centuries since we'd used them.

On the screen of the computer was a game. The object of the game was to spot the errors in a primitive symbolic language and correct them. Of course, before I could play I had to make sense of the system. But that was simple enough.

Once I understood the system, it was easy to spot the errors. I quickly rewrote it to make sense out of it.

<I win,> I said to myself.

"Hello?"

I turned around. It was an older human. He was paler than Marco, but other features were similar.

Marco had warned me to say nothing to his father but "yes" and "no."

"No," I said to Marco's father.

"I'm Marco's dad. Are you a friend of his?"

"Yes."

"What's your name?"

"No," I answered.

"Your name is 'No'?"

"Yes."

"That's an unusual name, isn't it?"

"No."

"It's not?"

65

"Yes."

"Yes, it's not an unusual name?"

"No."

"Now I'm totally confused."

"Yes."

Marco's father stared at me. Then, in a loud voice he yelled, "Hey, Marco? Marco? Would you . . . um . . . your friend is here. Your friend 'No' is here."

"No," I said.

"Yes, that's what I said."

Marco came running down the stairs. "Whoa!" he cried. "Um, Dad! You met my friend?"

"No?" Marco's father said.

"What?" Marco asked.

Marco's father shook his head. "I must be getting old. I don't understand you kids."

"Yes," I offered.

After that, we went to the bookstore.

CHAPTER 9

Books are an amazing human invention. They allow instant access to information simply by turning pieces of paper. They are much faster to use than computers. Surprisingly, humans invented books before computers. They do many things backward.
— **From the Earth Diary of Aximili-Esgarrouth-Isthill**

It was evening of the next day. I was in the woods. I was reading a book. The book was called the *World Almanac*. Did you know that twelve percent of households have a dehumidifier? Did you know that a sheep can live for twenty years? Did you know that humans used to believe the sun orbited Earth?

It's a wonderful book.

The book told me many useful things. It took humans only sixty-six years to go from inventing the first flying machine to landing on the moon. It took Andalites almost three times as long.

Humans are a very clever species. Someday,

if they survive, they could be one of the great races of the galaxy.

Of course, Andalites will always be greater.

I was standing by the stream, with one hoof in the water, drinking, when my stalk eyes saw a swift shadow falling from the sky.

Tobias opened his wings and shot just over my head. <Ax! Everyone is looking for you. Stay right here. I have to get them.>

He had kept most of his speed, so he swiftly disappeared above the trees. But a moment later he was back, with four other large birds of prey following him.

Tobias took a position on a branch. The others landed on the ground. I knew then it was the other Animorphs.

They quickly began to demorph. Prince Jake grew out of a falcon's racing body. Rachel emerged from a huge bald eagle. Cassie and Marco had both acquired osprey morphs, and were now becoming human again.

I felt a tingling of worry. They had obviously been searching for me, and were in a hurry.

<What is the matter?> I asked.

<What's the *matter*?> Marco demanded. <You're asking what's the matter? I'll tell —>

But just at that point, Marco crossed the line from thought-speaking morph back to human.

His human mouth was still a beak, however, so he just squawked.

I watched Cassie as she made the change. Cassie is a natural *estreen*: a person with an ability to make morphing almost artistic. On my planet it is an art form. There are professional *estreens* who change shape in fantastic, beautiful ways.

Cassie was not a professional, but she had the talent. As she morphed, she formed pleasant shapes. For a while she had an enlarged osprey's head, as large as a human head, and vast wings attached to a human body.

When the others morph, they are much less subtle. For them, human parts simply ooze out, while feathers melt away. It is very unappealing. The humans find it frightening and disgusting as well, I believe. And they even recognize that Cassie has a talent for morphing.

"What did you *do*?!" Marco's human mouth had reappeared.

<I don't understand the question.>

"My dad's computer. You did something to it, didn't you?"

<I . . . I merely played the game.>

"Game? GAME?! That was no game, that was my dad's work!"

<No. It was a game. You had to find the errors

69

in the instructions.> Suddenly an idea occurred to me. <Oh, I understand. Your father designs games for children.>

Cassie started to laugh, then silenced herself.

"No, Ax, he writes software programs for high-tech uses. He was working with astronomers at the observatory. They were designing a program for aiming the radio telescope at the new observatory."

I nodded, as I had seen humans do. <Yes, it could be used for that purpose. But it was so obviously full of errors . . . I assumed it was a child's game.>

"If you say 'game' again, I swear I'm going to punch you," Marco said.

Prince Jake put his hand on Marco's shoulder. "What Marco means is, it was not a game, Ax. His father is going nuts about it."

"My dad says you may have created some whole new branch of computer software, plus, at the same time, opened up new ways to do astronomy. He showed it to the guys at the observatory. They are totally losing it! They're talking about Nobel prizes! I had to convince my dad it was just an accident. I told him you were an idiot, and you were not the next Einstein."

<Einstein. Yes. I read about him in the *World Almanac*. He was the first human to realize that matter and energy —>

"Ax!" Rachel exploded. "Are you not getting this? What if some Controller hears about this new software? Don't you think they might guess it was an *Andalite* who came up with it?"

It hit me quite suddenly. She was right. If those equations were supposed to be real, not a game, but *real* . . . Then I had just pushed human science ahead by a century. Maybe more.

"I think he just got it," Marco said sarcastically.

<What is a radio telescope?> I asked Marco.

He shrugged. "Like I would know? What am I, a science teacher?"

"A radio telescope is a telescope that sees by picking up radio waves and other radiation from outer space," Cassie said.

Marco gave her an incredulous look.

"Not all of us sleep through science class, Marco," Cassie said.

<I see. A primitive sensor. Yes, that would make sense. Of course, with the changes I made . . .>

"What?" Marco snapped. "What about the changes you made?"

<The changes I made would only . . .>

Suddenly I stopped. The truth . . . the *whole* truth . . . was beginning to dawn on me. A radio telescope? A huge, high-powered collector of broad-spectrum energy?

71

My mind raced through memories of classes from a long time ago. I could almost picture my teacher explaining . . . yes. Yes! With the right adjustments, the right software . . . Yes, I could bounce the collected energy back, focus it, modulate it with my own mind, and . . .

And break into Z-space. Zero-space.

I could use the system to send messages through Z-space! I could communicate with my own world!

I felt it as a blow that made me weak. It was true. I could use that radio telescope to call my home world. To call my people. My family.

I don't think I had ever admitted, till that moment, just how much I wanted to see another Andalite.

"Ax, what are you hiding *now*?!" Rachel demanded.

I tried to concentrate on her question. But my mind was spinning. It made me feel weak. I could contact my home planet. I *could*.

But at the same time, there was another truth: I had to destroy this technology. I had broken the law of *Seerow's Kindness*. I had given the humans a huge advance in technology!

"Ax, Rachel asked you a question," Prince Jake said tersely. "What is this? What's up with you?"

My duty was clear. I could not tell my human

friends what I had done. I had to erase the damage.

But before I did that . . . would it be wrong to
contact my family? Would it be so wrong to once
again see them?

<I am not hiding anything,> I lied. <Nothing
at all.>

CHAPTER 10

They left, and I ate. I feed at dark whenever possible. It is not the way I would do it at home, but I must always be very careful not to be seen.

When I run in the open spaces it must either be dark, or Tobias must watch over me.

My friends tell me that from a distance I look like a normal Earth animal. A deer, or perhaps a small horse. But if any human saw me clearly, he would immediately know that I am not an Earth species.

So I eat at night, running wildly through the open grassy fields where Cassie's farm meets the edge of the forest. I run beneath a single moon, so different from the moons of my own world. The moon of Earth rises and sets. On some nights it cannot be seen at all. There are always at least two moons in our sky. And when all four moons are in the night sky, it is nearly as bright as day.

Home. Billions of miles away. Sometimes I hurt from thinking about my home. A warrior has to overcome that. But on nights when I stood alone in the forest, or ran alone in the fields, I couldn't help but think of home.

And now it was worse. So much worse, thinking that I could talk to them, if I really wanted to.

I could turn the humans' radio telescope into a Z-space communicator. But if I did, I would have broken our own law. I would have given the humans an advanced technology.

I couldn't do it. I wasn't Elfangor. I couldn't just decide to break the law of *Seerow's Kindness*.

And yet, in the back of my mind, there was another thought. I had already accidentally transferred the software to the humans. It was an accident, so I hadn't broken the rules. And if I went to the observatory to wipe out the software . . . I would actually be doing the right thing.

I could go to the observatory and erase the software. But before I erased it, I could use it to call my home. Would that be wrong?

In my memory I saw myself with my father and mother. And Elfangor was there, too. He was alive in my memory.

I remember when I was very little and Elfangor, who was already a great warrior, came home on leave. I barely knew him. I'd seen his communications, but I'd never met him face-to-face. He had been away when I was born, off fighting the Yeerks.

But we went running together, just the two of us. Me all clumsy. Elfangor like some creature from an Andalite myth, so fast and so powerful.

It was kind of a shock to me. Until then, I guess I'd thought I was the most important person in the family. But it was hard to feel very important with Elfangor around.

He didn't say much to me. He didn't give me some "big brother" lecture. He was just himself. He talked to me the same way he talked to my parents. He never treated me like a younger Andalite, and that was great. After that, there was never any question in my mind what I wanted to be when I grew up: I wanted to be a warrior. I wanted to be like Elfangor.

And now he was gone. My parents might not even know. For sure they didn't know I was still alive.

I slowed my run. I was far across the fields. I could see the lights from Cassie's farm. Foolish! I was so wrapped up in my thoughts that I had grown careless.

I turned to head back toward the forest.

"You might as well hang around for a while," a voice said.

<Cassie?>

She loomed up from the darkness. How had I missed seeing her? I looked closer. Cassie began to change. She kept her own human face, but the ghostly gray-white mane of a horse. And her legs ended in hooves, not human feet.

<You morphed a horse,> I said.

As soon as she was fully human she responded. "I do that sometimes. I like running. But don't tell Jake. He'd be mad at me using morphing for personal things."

<I don't believe he would be angry,> I said. <I am no expert on humans, but I believe Prince Jake has a special affection for you.>

Cassie laughed quietly. "I doubt it. I'm just a friend. And a fellow Animorph."

<Then why do you sometimes hold hands and intertwine your fingers?>

"Oh . . . well, you weren't supposed to see that."

<Why not?>

"Um, it's kind of a long story," Cassie said. "Just forget it, okay? How is your study of humans going?"

<I have read the *World Almanac*.>

"So, what do you think?"

<I think humans are interesting.>

"Uh-huh. What do you *really* think?"

I hesitated. She seemed to want a more complete answer. But you can never be sure with humans. Often they become offended by small things.

<I think there is a second reason why the Yeerks wish to enslave your species,> I said.

"Aside from being able to have a lot of human hosts? Why?"

<They're afraid of you.>

"Afraid of us? Why?" She laughed. "Have you been reading all the stuff about wars? Humans aren't just about fighting wars. It may seem that way, but —"

<Every species fights wars,> I said. <In the past, Andalites made war on other Andalites. And the Hork-Bajir used to have a biological time clock that set them all warring every sixty-two years. As for the Taxxons . . . they are cannibals.>

"Yeah, well, we humans haven't been exactly perfect."

<Every species has something to be ashamed of,> I said. <Every species carries some terrible guilt.>

She looked closely at me. I could almost see her wondering whether I meant Andalites as well. But she decided not to ask that question. Instead she asked another. "So if it isn't the wars that bother you, what is it?"

<You discovered radioactivity in 1896. In 1945 you exploded an atomic weapon. Forty-nine years. In 1903 you flew for the first time. Sixty-six years later, you landed on your moon.>

"You really did read the *World Almanac,* didn't you?" Cassie said with a smile. "You're saying we do things quickly?"

<I'm saying that if the Yeerks don't destroy you now, they know that fifty years from now, humans will be capable of faster-than-light travel. And a hundred years from now . . . who knows?>

"How long did it take you Andalites to do those things?"

<I . . . I don't remember,> I lied.

"I see," Cassie said. I believe her tone of voice is called "disappointed."

<I . . .> I hung my head. <I am bound by my oath as an Andalite warrior. We must never give Andalite technology to any other species, and we try not to, you know, talk about ourselves to other species.> It sounded pathetic, even to me.

"Not even if it might help us beat the Yeerks? But isn't that what your brother did, when he gave us the power to morph?"

I could not think of an answer. It was true, of course. Elfangor *had* broken our laws.

"Did I say something wrong?" Cassie asked.

<I'm not Elfangor,> I said finally. <I'm more like you. Just a young one. Elfangor was a great prince. My people might understand and forgive what Elfangor did, because he was an important person.>

"I see," Cassie said. "You know what? Why don't you morph to human and come inside? You could meet my mom and dad. We're just about to have dinner."

<I have eaten already.>

Cassie raised one eyebrow. "You've eaten, huh?" She seemed about to ask me a question, then decided against it. "Okay, but you could still come in. You don't have to eat much. Just hang out. Come on, it would do you good."

<Do me good? Do I seem ill?>

"No. Just lonely. You seem very lonely."

The word pierced me. I was surprised how much it hurt.

Yes, I was lonely. But I didn't think the humans knew.

<How would you explain to your family who I was?>

Cassie shrugged. "You morphed Jake once, right? So be Jake."

CHAPTER 11

Humans have very odd tastes. They think their music is beautiful. They are wrong. It is awful. All of it. And they completely ignore their greatest accomplishments: the cinnamon bun, the Snickers bar, the hot pepper, and the refreshing beverage called vinegar.
— **From the Earth Diary of Aximili-Esgarrouth-Isthill**

Being in Prince Jake's body is no different from being in my regular human morph. Except that it is slightly larger. Since the morph was formed from his DNA, I looked exactly like him. Cassie insisted I borrow a garment called "overalls" and a pair of boots from her barn before entering her home. Humans are very particular about clothing. I still do not understand why.

"Hi, Jake. Cassie talk you into helping her muck out the barn again?" Cassie's father asked me as I walked into her house.

He was a male — as all human fathers are.

81

His hair was dark brown, but it seemed to have been removed from much of his head. He wore round transparent lenses on his face which, I am told, are for correcting faulty vision. His complexion is darker. He had the usual number of legs and arms.

"No," I said. "She asked me to eat your food. Food. Ood-duh."

"Well, *someone* has to eat it. Might as well be you who suffers. I cooked tonight. Made my world-famous chili."

Cassie's eyes suddenly widened. She looked frightened. "Oh. Chili? Um, Jake said he wasn't really hungry. He already ate."

"Is chili a very frightening food?" I asked Cassie.

Her father grinned. "Mine is."

"Is that Jake I hear out there?" someone called from the next room. A female appeared who I assumed was Cassie's mother. She had dark hair, but much more of it than Cassie's father. Her hair had not been removed.

She stuck her two arms in my direction and walked toward me. "Oh, you just get more handsome every time I see you, Jake." She wrapped her two arms around me and squeezed me briefly. Then she released me. "Are you staying for some of the Chili of Doom?"

"Yes, I asked him to join us," Cassie said. "But he's not very hungry. In fact, he just ate. So he probably won't want any chili."

Cassie's mother smiled at Cassie's father. "Isn't it just precious the way she tries to protect him?"

"Too late," Cassie's father said. "He's trapped now. There is no escape."

In order to eat we had to sit down in front of a table. I had done this before while impersonating Prince Jake at Prince Jake's home. So I knew how to do it. I knew what a fork was. Also a spoon and a knife.

I discovered that chili is brown and red. It contains several ingredients and smells a lot. There was also something called jalapeño corn bread. And there was a bowl of pieces of different fruits.

After so many warnings, I was very nervous about tasting the chili. But I sensed that Cassie's father would be offended if I did not try some. So I ate a spoonful.

I think that as long as I live, I will never forget that experience.

The chili was hot in temperature. But it was also hot in a totally new way.

The tastebuds of my human tongue seemed to explode! They burned with an intensity of flavor like nothing I'd tasted before or since. Every nerve in my body seemed to tingle. Water dribbled from the tiny ducts beside my eyes.

It was not as wonderful as chocolate. But it was intense! So incredibly intense!

Oh! An Andalite would never understand. This was what being human was all about. Taste! The glory of it. The incredible wonder of it.

"This is a wonderful food!" I cried.

"Excuse me?" Cassie's mother said.

"Ah HAH! At last. Someone who understands the joy of hot food!" Cassie's father cried.

I realized I had eaten my entire bowl of that marvelous chili. I wanted more. That taste! That feeling! I wanted more!

"There's plenty more," Cassie's father said. He filled my bowl again.

"Um, Jake?" Cassie said. "You really don't have to eat that much."

"I'll eat yours!" I cried.

My eyes were bulging from my head. My skin was tingling. My stomach was making sounds. But still, I wanted more.

"I love this kid," Cassie's father said. "I wonder if his parents would let us adopt him. Jake, you are a very discerning, intelligent young man."

"He's insane," Cassie's mother said. "There's no other explanation."

Suddenly, I felt a sharp pain in my leg. I suspected that Cassie had kicked me under the table. I looked at her. She smiled sweetly, and then kicked me again.

"That's probably enough chili," she said. She was staring at me in a very direct way.

"Yes. That is enough chili," I agreed. I pushed the bowl away. "Chili. Ili. Chee-lee."

"I used habanero chilies," Cassie's father said. "The hottest substance known to man."

"Not as hot as the temperature created during nuclear fusion," I pointed out.

"So how is school, Jake?" Cassie's mother asked.

I knew what this activity was. This was called "making conversation." The rules were that each person would ask the other person a question.

"It is fine. And how is your work caring for animals?"

"Same old, same old," Cassie's mother said. "Although we are about to have some new camel babies."

Cassie's mother is a veterinarian at the zoo, a place where nonhuman animals are kept.

"So, Jake, you think the Bulls are going all the way again this year?" Cassie's father asked.

I could tell that Cassie was growing tense. She was afraid that I would not understand the question. But thanks to my reading of the *World Almanac,* I knew the "Bulls" were a sports team.

"Yes," I answered. "They can go all the way."

Then, it was my turn to ask a question. That is how "making conversation" works. "So, did you know that the cream separator was invented in 1878?"

Apparently, they did not know. Cassie, her mother, and her father all stared at me in surprise.

After that, we watched television for a while. It was a fictional depiction of a family. I watched it, and watched Cassie and her parents.

A human family was a good thing to learn about. I had seen Prince Jake's family. And now I was seeing Cassie's family. They are different in some ways. For example, Prince Jake's family performs a brief religious ritual before they eat. Cassie's family does not. And in Prince Jake's family, the father falls asleep while watching television. In Cassie's family, it was her mother who began to fall asleep.

"I must go," I told Cassie. "It has been almost two of your hours."

Cassie's mother revived long enough to say that I was crazy, but I was "still so cute."

Her father winked his left eye at me and waved as I left. Then he laughed at something from the television.

Outside in the cool evening air, Cassie sighed heavily. "Well, we got through that without it being too much of a disaster. Come on. I'll walk you out a ways, till you can morph back without being seen. By the way, here's a book for you, since you're done with the *World Almanac*. It's a book of quotes. Stuff that famous people said." She held it out for me to take.

"Thank you," I said.

I felt strange walking into the dark. Walking away from Cassie's house. Strange. As if it were cold out, although it wasn't.

"So what did you think of my parents?" Cassie asked.

"I liked them," I said. "But why has your father removed the hair from his head? Hair. Hay-yer. I meant to ask him, but forgot."

"He's going bald," Cassie said. "It's probably better not to mention it. It's a normal thing for humans. But some people get sensitive about it."

"Ah, yes. My father's hooves are getting dull. It's normal as well, but he doesn't like to talk about it."

"What's your father like? And your mother?"

"They are . . . just normal parents. They are very nice. They are . . ."

"Go on."

"My throat feels strange," I said. "Like there is an obstruction. I am having difficulty speaking. Ing. Is this normal?"

Cassie put her arm beneath mine. "You miss them. That's normal."

"An Andalite warrior may spend many years in space, far from his home and family. That's normal."

"Ax. You said it yourself. You may be an Andalite warrior, but you're still a kid, too."

I stopped walking. I was far from the light of the house. I could change back into my own shape without being seen. I realized I was looking up at the stars.

"Where are they?" Cassie asked, following the direction of my gaze. "If you're allowed to tell me that."

I pointed with my human fingers at the quadrant of space where my home star twinkled. "There."

I watched that star as I melted out of my human form and returned to my true Andalite body.

"Ax, you know that Jake and Tobias and me, and even Rachel and Marco, we all care about you. You know that, right? You're not just some alien to us."

<Thank you for the chili,> I said. <It was wonderful.>

Once more an Andalite, I ran for the forest.

CHAPTER 12

I spent part of the night reading the book of quotes. I should have been resting, but I felt disturbed.

More and more I thought of how easily I could turn the radio telescope at the observatory into a Z-space transmitter. The idea of contacting my parents filled me with sadness and longing.

<They could tell me what to do,> I thought. <They could give me instructions.>

And in another part of my mind I thought, <Wouldn't they be proud that I was fighting on against the Yeerks? They would all say, "He's another Elfangor. A hero.">

I'm not proud that I was thinking that. But I have to tell the truth. And the truth was, I wanted everyone back home to think I was being very brave, all alone on Earth.

Already in my mind a plan was taking shape.

I found a quiet place and prepared to sleep. I closed my main eyes, leaving only my stalk eyes open to look for danger. I relaxed my tail until it touched the ground.

Lonely.

Yes, it was lonely to sleep in a forest on a planet far from home. It was lonely to be the only one of my kind.

It was lonely knowing that Cassie was asleep in her home, and Marco in his, and Rachel and Jake. All had homes.

All but me. And Tobias.

Tobias. He would understand. But would he help me? If I did what I was planning, would he help? And could I trust him?

I raised my tail and opened my main eyes. I knew the place where Tobias slept. I found him easily. He stood with his sharp talons wrapped around a branch.

<Tobias?> I called.

<Huh? What? Ax? What's the matter?>

<Nothing is the matter. But . . . I have a question.>

<I hope it's a good one. I was sleeping.>

<Tobias. Are you my friend?>

<That's what you woke me up to ask?> He opened his wings and seemed to be stretching. <Ax, we are the two strangest creatures on this planet: a freaky, four-eyed, half-deer, half-scorpion, centaur-looking alien, and a bird with the mind of a person. We've fought side by side. We've been nearly killed several times. Of course I'm your friend.>

It surprised me that he would answer so quickly. As if there was never any doubt what the answer would be. <That's good,> I said. <Will you keep a secret? Even from Prince Jake? Even from Rachel?>

Tobias was silent for a while. <Is it something that would hurt my friends?>

<No.>

<Then I'd keep a secret,> Tobias said. <I swear.>

<What do you swear by, Tobias? I have to be sure. What promise would you *never* break?>

<Ax, you know I was there when your brother was killed.>

<Yes. I know. You were the last one to leave him.>

<Yeah. I don't know why,> Tobias said. <But something about him . . . I can't explain it, but I was drawn to him. I wanted to listen to him. I wanted to hear everything he said. It was like . . .

91

like he was a magnet or something. Like I couldn't pull away. Until he ordered me to leave. I can't explain it.>

<You don't need to explain,> I said softly. Even here, among aliens, Elfangor was the hero.

<You asked what I'd swear by. I'll swear by him. By Prince Elfangor.>

And so, I told Tobias of my plan.

CHAPTER 13

> "E.T. phone home." When I found that sentence in Cassie's book of human quotes, it surprised me. To be honest, it almost scared me. It was as if it were written just for me. I thought maybe, somehow, my human friends had discovered my plan and written it there.
> — **From the Earth Diary of Aximili-Esgarrouth-Isthill**

The sun was just coming up over planet Earth.

I performed the morning ritual, as I always did. But I was especially impatient this morning. I knew Tobias was hunting a morning meal and would be back as soon as he had finished eating some unfortunate mouse or shrew.

<Freedom is my only cause. Duty to the people, my only guide. Obedience to my prince, my only glory.>

When Tobias returned from the hunt, we would go. He would lead me to the observatory,

93

to the great radio telescope. And, with luck, I would be able to call my home.

<I, Aximili-Esgarrouth-Isthill, Andalite warrior, offer my life.>

With my stalk eyes I saw a hawk swoop low overhead. Tobias rested on a branch. He focused his fierce hawk's eyes on me. <Are you done?>

<Yes. The ritual is complete.>

<Great. Because it is a beautiful day for flying. Thermals like you wouldn't believe. And a sweet little ground breeze for easy takeoff.>

<Tobias, you understand that you don't have to do this,> I said. <There may be danger.>

<Yeah, yeah. Come on, Ax. Let's go, already.>

I often go flying with Tobias. The bird morph I have is called a northern harrier. It is a type of hawk, about the same size as Tobias's red-tail. Tobias's feathers are mostly brown and light tan, while the harrier's are mostly gray and white.

I controlled my excitement and worry, and focused on making the change.

The harrier morph is always strange. For one thing, there is a great difference in size between an Andalite and a bird, even a large bird.

The first sensation was one of falling, as I shrank rapidly.

My stalk eyes went blind and wings grew out of my front legs, which is very awkward. It causes me to fall forward onto the ground, since I cannot stand on my hind legs alone.

Besides, my hind legs were busy shriveling down into the tiny yellow, scaly bird legs. And my tail was shrinking and splitting into dozens of long tail feathers.

Harriers also have mouths, like humans. Only these mouths are useless for speech, and have very little ability to taste. On the other hand, they are wonderful natural weapons. They are razor-sharp, and curved down into a ripping, tearing hook.

And the talons are excellent. I had long admired Tobias's use of his talons. He can swoop fast and low, just a few feet above the ground, and snatch up a mouse or small rabbit with those talons.

As I watched, the blue and tan fur of my own body was replaced by silvery gray feathers. The fur melted away to show the underlying flesh, and then the flesh became patterned with the millions of individual ribs of feathers.

I was used to the mind of the harrier, so I had learned to control its instincts. Its instincts were more forceful than those in the brains of humans.

<I've been meaning to ask you, Ax,> Tobias said. <Not to diss you or anything, but why is it

95

that Cassie is better at morphing than you are? I mean, you're an Andalite. But you look just as creepy as Jake or Rachel when you do it.>

<Cassie has talent,> I said a little grumpily. <Morphing does not happen to be my talent.>

<Oh. You ready to fly?>

I checked. I opened my wings to their full three-and-a-half-foot spread. I flicked my tail feathers. I focused my laserlike hawk's eyes on a far distant tree and was able to see individual ants crawling up its trunk.

I listened to the forest with the harrier's superior hearing. I could hear the insects beneath the pine needles. I could hear a squirrel chewing open a nut. I could hear Tobias's heart beating.

I turned into the breeze and opened my wings. I flapped several times and lifted my legs clear of the ground. The breeze caught me and I was off.

Even with the breeze, I had to flap hard to get as high as the treetops. Tobias was already several dozen feet above me. But then, Tobias has had a great deal of practice.

I swept just above the treetops, flapping and soaring. The sun was beating down on the treetops and heat waves were rising. I caught the updraft and shot higher. I was two hundred feet up in just seconds.

I could see Cassie's farm now. And as I circled to use the updraft for more altitude, I could see all the familiar landmarks: the homes of the others. The mall. The school.

<Stick with me,> Tobias said. <We'll follow the water's edge. The observatory is north along the coast. About an hour's flying time.>

We reached the ocean. There were cliffs along the shore, and here the real thermals rose up. A thermal is an updraft of heated air. Flying into one is like flying into an elevator or drop shaft. The updraft catches your wings and lifts you up and up and up.

It is a fantastic, giddy, wild feeling.

I wheeled and turned to stay within the thermal, following Tobias higher and higher.

<We want to get above the gulls,> Tobias instructed. <Sometimes seagulls get obnoxious. They'll swarm a hawk if they're in the wrong mood.>

It was exhilarating. We were thousands of feet above the ground. Down below, humans lay on the beach wearing less clothing than usual. Clothing is a strange human habit. They must wear it all the time. Except at the beach, when they may wear less.

I don't understand this. The *World Almanac* had no explanation. Although I did know that the United States imported 36.7 billion dollars' worth of clothing.

97

<Keep an eye on that guy up there,> Tobias said.

<Where? What?> I asked, shaken out of my dreamy thoughts.

<A peregrine falcon. He's probably looking to pick off a few tasty seagulls. But he may decide we look more tender. He's small but fast. Mean, too.>

I decided to keep an eye on the falcon. Earth is a dangerous, wild place. At least, if you're a bird.

I thought it must be terrible sometimes for Tobias. He lives in fear of things that no human would need to fear. He has lost his position at the top of the food chain of Earth. Hawks are predators, but they are also prey. Yet he seemed to have accepted his fate. Was it possible he even preferred being a hawk? Was that why he never asked me why I might know about him being a *nothlit?*

Or did he think I would refuse to answer, or worse yet, lie?

Fortunately, the falcon ignored us and we flew on, following the coastline. Soon we had left the city behind. The beaches were gone, too. The coastline grew more rugged, with waves that crashed in explosions of foam against jagged broken rocks.

A single road wound along the coast below us.

There were cars on it, but few buildings. Then, in the distance, I saw a large white structure.

Actually, several structures. There was a tall building with a dome top. And arrayed around it in various positions were several large white flattened bowls. It took me several seconds to figure out their purpose.

<That's the radio telescope?> I laughed. <You're still using dish arrays?>

<Won't they work for . . . for whatever it is you're doing?> Tobias asked.

<Oh, yes, they should work. If I can gain access to the computers, they should work very well. It's just that they're so primitive.>

<I don't suppose you want to tell me what we're doing, huh?>

<Doing? We're flying,> I said.

<Very funny. Suddenly you have a sense of humor. Great.>

CHAPTER 14

< The large building with the dome?> I asked Tobias as I swept above the observatory. <Is that where the computers would be?>

<Maybe. That's where they have the regular telescope, I think. But they may have the control centers and computers there, too.>

I looked with my incredible hawk vision. There was a huge, rectangular opening in the top of the dome. Inside I could see a vast circle of glass. I laughed in recognition. <A telescope? An actual *optical* telescope? What can they possibly believe *that* will show them?>

<It will show them a red-tail and a harrier flying around together, looking like lost tourists,>

Tobias said. <According to Marco, this place isn't really operating yet. So I don't know how many people will be around. But we need to find a place to land, so you can morph into something useful, and do . . . whatever.>

<Tobias. Is that sarcasm? The way you ask me what I'm doing?>

<No, it's not sarcasm. I think it's called being snide.>

<Ah. Thanks for explaining. Why not fly straight into the dome?> I asked.

<Why not?> Tobias agreed. He led the way down.

We dived at high speed, rocketing down through the air. The brilliant white dome rushed up at us. I shot through the open rectangle and banked sharply right.

It was much darker inside than outside. Below me was the incredibly long tube of the telescope.

<I see doors down below. Those are probably offices,> Tobias said. <They'll probably have computers in all the offices. If we can find one that's empty.>

<Yes. That would be good. But I will need fingers.>

<For . . .>

<For whatever it is I'm doing,> I said.

101

We circled swiftly around the inside of the dome. As I flew, I kept expecting to see humans below. But none ever appeared.

<This place is awfully empty,> Tobias said.

<Yes. It seems almost abandoned,> I agreed. <Tobias, I am going down. My morph time is running short. Now is when I should go on alone.>

<Yeah. Gotcha. Good luck, Ax-man. Whatever you're doing, be careful.>

Tobias swept up and out of the dome. I was alone.

I drifted down toward the floor. Down and down, to land on a table. There was a computer console workstation. But no humans in sight.

I saw an open door leading to what seemed to be a dark and empty office. I flapped my wings twice and was inside.

Harrier eyes, like hawk eyes, are adapted for daylight. They are not very good in the dark. But the harrier also has extremely good hearing. I dimly saw a desk and came to rest on it. Then I concentrated on listening.

I was alone in the room. I was certain of that. The only human sounds I heard came through the walls.

Conversation. I could not make out the sounds, but they all seemed to be concentrated in one area.

<Ax can — hear me?>

It was Tobias. His thought-speech was faint.

<Just barely,> I answered.

<I'm outside. I'm loo — ing —— a window —— here. I see — ven —— in a room. —— like some kind of meeting.>

<Yes, I can hear them,> I said. <Can you keep watch over them? Let me know if they come this way?>

<Yeah. If any —— leaves the — ting, I'll know —— ,> Tobias said.

<I can barely hear you,> I said. <I'm going to morph.>

<Can't —— very well, but go ——>

My plan was to morph to my normal Andalite form, then quickly move into my human morph, just in case any humans saw me. But I was tired from the flight. And morphing is very tiring. Especially quick morphing. And if I had to make a quick escape it would mean passing through my Andalite body to move back to harrier.

I would never be able to handle that many changes in a short time. I decided to risk staying in Andalite form.

Besides . . . if it worked and I reached my home, I wanted my parents to know me when they saw me.

I began the demorphing. I could only hope that Tobias would be able to give me enough warning.

Even though I loved being a bird, it was a good feeling when my tail began to form again. An Andalite without a tail is just sad.

And no matter how powerful a hawk's eyes may be, they can still only look in one direction at a time. As my stalk eyes reformed, I breathed a sigh of relief. I could once again see in all directions.

There was no computer in the office. I was very annoyed by that fact. It meant I would have to go back into the observatory to use the computer there.

My hooves slipped on the polished floor. I swung my eyes in every direction, keeping a sharp lookout.

I pushed the chair away from the computer workstation. I began typing on the antique keyboard. The screen asked me for a password.

<Password?> I laughed. I disabled the security system and confirmed that Marco's father's new software was already in place.

Good. That would make it easier. As quickly as I could, I wrote in a virus that would swiftly transform the software that controlled the radio telescope.

Since humans had no awareness of Zerospace, they did not understand that a powerful radio receiver could be tuned in such a way as to create a Z-space vacuum and open a cross-dimensional gateway.

Once I had opened a small hole in Z-space, it was child's play to use the same receivers to modulate and reflect the background radiation into a coherent signal. The hard part would be using thought-speech to control the signal. That would take absolute concentration.

<Still —— out here,> Tobias said.

I hoped the word I couldn't hear was "okay."

It took about ten Earth minutes to adjust the radio telescope. Ten minutes, and I had moved human science ahead by a century or so.

Ten minutes to completely violate Andalite law.

I was done. The system was ready.

I pressed the "enter" key.

The thousands of lines of computer language disappeared from the computer's screen.

The screen went blank.

I focused my mind as sharply as I could. I pictured the coherent signal. I pictured that beam going through my own head.

<Andalite Home,> I thought. <Andalite Home.>

The screen flickered.

A face appeared. It was a hard, suspicious face. But it was an Andalite face.

<Who is this?> the Andalite demanded. <This is a high security link. You are not an authorized sender. State your name and location.>

<My name is Aximili-Esgarrouth-Isthill. Brother of Elfangor-Sirinial-Shamtul. Son of Noorlin-Sirinial-Cooraf and Forlay-Esgarrouth-Maheen.>

The Andalite stared at me. <Elfangor's brother?> he wondered. <What is your location?>

<My location is the planet called Earth.>

CHAPTER 15

<E arth!>

<Yes.>

<Is Prince Elfangor with you?>

For a moment my concentration wavered. I lost the signal. But then, I forced myself to focus. This was too important to let my emotions mess things up.

<Who are you?> I asked.

He looked surprised that I would ask. <I am Ithileran-Halas-Corain. Assistant to the Head of Planetary Communications.>

<Thank you. Ithileran, my brother's life . . . ended,> I said. <The Dome ship was destroyed. I am the only survivor.>

I could see that this was a surprise. Ithileran's

107

eyes were downcast, and he lowered his stalk eyes as well in a gesture of grief.

<Your brother was a great warrior. And I mourn also for the many other warriors aboard the Dome ship.>

<Elfangor was the greatest,> I said. <My family doesn't know he's dead. I would like you to connect me with them. I could get interrupted any minute.>

<I will do that. As soon as your family is found, I will connect you. But first, give me your report, *aristh* Aximili.>

I tried to quickly organize my thoughts. <The Yeerks are here in force. There is at least one mother ship. Also one Blade ship belonging to Visser Three, and numerous Bug fighters. The humans are unaware of the invasion. I do not know how many humans have been made into Controllers, but there must be thousands, at least.>

I took a deep breath, and tried to hold onto my concentration. How much should I tell Ithileran?

<Then Earth is lost to the Yeerks?>

<No!> I said sharply. <Earth is not lost. There is a small resistance. A few humans. Young . . . *arisths*, like me. I fight alongside them.>

<But surely there is no hope of victory?>

<We have hurt the Yeerks,> I said. <We have

destroyed the Kandrona that was in place on this planet.>

That got Ithileran's attention. That definitely got his attention. <You destroyed a Yeerk Kandrona? How did you manage that? You and a handful of human youths?>

It was time to tell him the full truth, or decide to lie.

<The humans . . . the humans have the power to morph,> I said. <Visser Three believes they are a small band of escaped Andalites. Earth has many strange animals, and with the morphing we use those species to attack the Yeerks.>

<Humans who morph? And how did humans come by this technology?>

<It was given to them. By Elfangor.>

Ithileran looked startled. His eyes darted to the side and then he abruptly disappeared from the screen. In his place stood another Andalite.

I was stunned. I instantly recognized the face.

He was very old, and yet his power seemed to vibrate through the screen, across all the light years that separated Earth from home.

Lirem-Arrepoth-Terrouss.

Head of the Council. Veteran of more battles than I could count. His appearance on the screen would have made me lose concentration, but I was too awed to dare.

109

<You know who I am?>

<Yes. Yes, um. Yes. Yes, I know you. I mean, I don't *know* you, but I know who you are.>

He ignored my babbling. <I mourn the loss of your brother and all aboard that ship. Now tell me: Did Elfangor break our laws and give technology to the humans?>

<Um, well . . . the humans were helpless. Our force had been destroyed. There was nothing to stand between the humans and total domination by the Yeerks. They needed some weapon.>

Lirem stared at me with a gaze that was known to make great princes tremble.

<And how have you come to contact us? This is a Z-space transmission.>

<I . . . I . . . I made some modifications to a primitive human device.>

<So, you *also* break the law. You also transfer technology to the humans.>

<The humans are not our enemies!> I said. I surprised myself by practically yelling. <They won't have a chance. These few humans are all that resist the Yeerks on this planet. Elfangor knew that. He did what he thought was right!>

To my surprise, Lirem did not tell me to be silent. But his eyes grew darker, his expression more serious than ever. Then he said, <*Aristh* Aximili, once before an Andalite did what he thought was the right thing. He transferred technology to a weak, backward species. He did it because he thought they should be able to travel to the stars. Do you know the name of that Andalite?>

<Prince Seerow,> I said.

<Prince Seerow. Yes. He was my first prince. Did you know that? Many centuries ago when I was an *aristh* like you.> Lirem looked hard at me. <Do you know what happened because of *Seerow's Kindness*?>

<Yes,> I said grimly. <Yes, I know. I have seen what happened because of *Seerow's Kindness*.>

For a moment no one spoke.

Then Lirem said, <Young Aximili, your brother Elfangor is a hero. The people need heroes in this endless war. I do not wish to tell the people that in the end, Elfangor broke the laws. There can be no forgiveness for a prince that breaks the laws. Unlike an *aristh*. So . . . I ask you to think again. Was it truly *Elfangor* who gave this technology to the humans?>

I couldn't believe what Lirem wanted me to say. He wanted me to lie. He wanted me to clear Elfangor.

<I . . . I was wrong when I said Elfangor did this,> I said, too shocked to argue. <It was . . . it was me. I gave the humans the morphing technology.>

Lirem continued. <Cut off from your prince,

111

alone, not yet trained, not yet a true warrior, you broke the laws, *aristh* Aximili. Is this true?>

<Yes,> I whispered bitterly.

<In the name of the council, I forgive your error,> Lirem said. <What's done is done. Perhaps . . . in some way I am too old to see, this may all work out for the best.>

<Yes,> I said blankly. Why had I done this? Why had I communicated with my home?

<*Aristh* Aximili-Esgarrouth-Isthill, you have done a brave thing, taking on this guilt. I know the temptation to go beyond the law when helping a brave people fight the Yeerks. I was an advisor to the Hork-Bajir. They were our allies, but they were not Andalites. They were not our people.>

<But . . .> I knew I should shut up. But part of me was getting angry. <But the Hork-Bajir ended up losing everything.>

Lirem's eyes were cold. <You are an Andalite. You are not a human. Obey our laws. I am giving you an order: Resist the Yeerks. But give the humans no information and no technology. Do you understand my order, *aristh* Aximili?>

<Yes.>

<The fleet is engaged in many parts of the galaxy. We are doing well against the Yeerks. But it will be some time before we can come to Earth. Fight the Yeerks. If you are half the hero your brother was, you will bring honor on your family.>

From what seemed like far away, I heard a faint voice in my head. <Ax ——— on the move. ——— guy. Think he ——— .>

But at that very moment, Lirem said, <Aximili, we have your father. He would like to speak to you.>

CHAPTER 16

<ᴴx —— you hear? —— there's ——————>

<Aximili-kala,> my father said. It was his nickname for me.

I couldn't believe it was really him. <Yes, Father. It's me. It's me, Aximili. I'm on Earth. I don't know how long I can talk, not long.>

<Is your brother there?>

It came so quickly, the question I dreaded. I almost lost the contact. I desperately wanted to see my father's face and listen to his words. But at the same time, I did not want to tell him that his oldest son was gone.

And there was another thing I did not want to tell him.

<Elfangor,> my father said. <Is he . . .>

<Father. Elfangor is . . . he was killed.>

My father looked like someone had punched him. He rocked back.

I looked away. I had tried so hard not to think about Elfangor being gone. Somehow it wasn't real till this moment. Seeing my father's pain made me feel my own.

<Did he die well?> my father asked. The question is part of the ritual of death. It was the question he had to ask.

<He died in the service of his people, defending freedom,> I said. This also was part of the ritual.

My father nodded. <And has his death been avenged?>

This was the part I had feared. <No, Father.>

My father looked up at me. <You are now the eldest son. The burden of revenge is on you. Do you know his killer?>

<Yes.>

<And does his killer still live?>

<Yes.>

<And do you, Aximili, take up the burden of avenging your brother's death?>

<Yes.>

The ritual was complete. We had both said all the things we were supposed to say.

<I am so relieved to see that you are still well,> my father said.

115

<Yes. I . . . I wanted to see you,> I said. <I couldn't —>

The connection was broken. Instantly, totally. I was staring at a blank screen.

"Sorry, but you were breaking my heart," a human voice sneered. "I *had* to cut you off."

I spun around. A human! He was thirty feet away.

And he was holding a weapon, pointing it at me.

Only slowly did I realize that it was no human gun. The weapon in his hand was a Dracon beam. Standard Yeerk issue.

"You and I have a lot to talk about, Andalite. Quite a lot."

I was frozen. I could not move. The human-Controller was too far away for me to hit with my tail.

"Don't try it, Andalite," he sneered. "I'll fry you before you can even twitch that tail of yours."

But then . . .

"Tseeeeeeeeeerrr!"

Tobias dived from the top of the dome at full speed, wings swept back, talons raked forward. He aimed for the man's face.

The man threw up his arm. Talons raked the bare flesh of his forearm, leaving red slashes behind. But the man had held on to the Dracon beam. Tobias flew past. Shreds of the human's shirt hung from his talons.

I leapt forward. Too late!

"Freeze! I don't want to kill either of you, Andalites, but I will if I have to!" the man snapped.

Tobias swooped away to perch on the huge telescope itself.

"I just want to talk," the human-Controller said.

<You're the one holding the Dracon beam,> I pointed out.

Then, he did something that amazed me. He knelt down and placed the Dracon beam on the floor. He kicked it aside. The weapon went skittering across the polished floor.

"Now I'm at your mercy, Andalite," he said. "You can use that tail of yours. Or you can listen to what I have to say."

With my stalk eyes I glanced up and saw Tobias.

<It's up to you, Ax,> Tobias said. <This is *your* party.>

<Speak, then,> I said to the human-Controller.

"My name is Gary Kozlar," he said.

<Don't waste my time,> I snapped, trying to sound strong and unafraid. <That's a *human* name. That's the name of your host body. But I know what you really are.>

He nodded. "All right. My name is Eslin

117

three-five-nine. And you are Aximili, a young Andalite warrior-cadet. Brother of Beast Elfangor. You see, I heard the last few minutes of your touching conversation."

<Beast Elfangor? So that is the Yeerk name for my brother?>

"Your brother is dead," Eslin snapped. "And so is the one creature in all the galaxy that I cared about. Her name was Derane three-four-four. And do you know what they have in common, your brother and my Derane?"

<No. What does my brother have in common with a Yeerk?>

Eslin's human face twisted into an expression of rage. "They were both killed by the same being."

<Visser Three?>

"As I said, you and I have a lot in common, Andalite." He struggled to gain control over his human face, but his jaw was twitching as he explained. "You Andalite bandits did a lot of damage by destroying the Kandrona. There is widespread starvation. The most important Yeerks, those in vital positions, or those whom the Visser happens to favor, are being shuttled back and forth to the mother ship every three days. They get a minimal dose of Kandrona rays. Enough to keep them alive."

<Do you expect me to feel badly?> I asked.

"No, I expect the usual Andalite self-righteousness and hypocrisy from you," Eslin spat. "Andalites. The meddlers of the galaxy."

<Do not anger me, Yeerk. I said I would listen. I did not say I would let you spew Yeerk lies.>

Eslin made a grim smile. "I knew you'd come. As soon as I saw the new software, I said to myself, 'Aha, not the usual clumsy human effort, this.' An Andalite corrected this software. An Andalite who wanted to use the radio telescope as a Z-space transmitter. I've been waiting for you. I knew you'd come."

<And here I am,> I said. I felt like a fool. Of course the Yeerks would have one of their own people in a position at the observatory. It was obvious. I had been an idiot. An idiot!

"My Derane . . . we came from the same pool. We went through training together. She and I . . . we had been together for a long time. We were very close. She understood me. But I had this important post at the observatory, while Derane was given a minor post. When you Andalite bandits destroyed the ground-based Kandrona, Visser Three moved quickly. He said everyone would survive. He said he had found a way. But he lied. Too many Yeerks, not enough Kandrona

119

rays. It was simple division. So he shuttled so-called important Controllers up to the mother ship. And the rest . . .

Eslin seemed to notice the bloody gashes on his arm for the first time. He touched them gingerly. "You Andalites must love this planet. So many nasty species for you to morph."

<Was your Derane one of the ones killed?>

"She was 'expendable,'" Eslin said. Then he smiled. "I've had some small revenge already. The Visser's favorites are shuttled up to the mother ship every three days to feed. I sabotaged one of the shuttles. That threw off the feeding schedule. Now some of the Visser's friends are starving and dying. Like my Derane died."

<That's why we're starting to see Controllers losing it,> Tobias said privately to me. <That's why it took so long. Visser Three had it under control till this guy messed with his plan.>

<Are you finished, Eslin?> I asked him. <I've heard your story. Is there a point to it?>

"Ah. You want the point of the story. Yes, of course. The point. The point is this: Visser Three inhabits an Andalite body. And sometimes he feeds like an Andalite."

<What's that mean?> Tobias asked me.

"He feeds like an Andalite, almost alone. He has guards of course, but they stay back. He is vulnerable. Vulnerable. And I know the place where he feeds."

<Why are you telling me this, Yeerk?>

"Why?" He bared his human teeth in a grimace of rage. "Because I want him *dead*. I want Visser Three dead! He killed my Derane. He killed the only one in the galaxy I have ever had feelings for. *He* did it. And I want him to pay with his life, the foul, half-Andalite scum. I want him DEAD!"

He calmed himself down, at least a little. He pulled a small piece of paper from his pocket. He placed it on the desk. "Time and place," he said. "You have a day to prepare."

<This could be a trap.>

Eslin sneered. "I could have killed you here. You have your duty, Andalite. The burden of revenge. Your brother's killer. Your greatest enemy. You Andalites are great ones for duty. So do your duty, Andalite."

CHAPTER 17

It is very difficult to be in human morph and remember that you are not one of them. That their pain is not your pain. It is hard to remain apart. Sometimes very hard.
— **From the Earth Diary of Aximili-Esgarrouth-Isthill**

That same evening, Prince Jake called a meeting in Cassie's barn.

My first thought was that Tobias had told the others about my trip to the observatory. Of course, Tobias still did not know that I had communicated with my home. But he did know all about Eslin's plan to kill Visser Three.

Cassie's barn is also called the Wildlife Rehabilitation Clinic. She and her father use it to rescue wild animals who are injured or sick. There are always dozens of animals in cages: skunks, foxes, raccoons, birds of all types. Many are bandaged.

It's strange, the relationship humans have to the other animals on Earth. Some animals they seem to have an enormous amount of emotion for. Others they hate. I think it has to do with the thing called "cuteness." But I've never understood the concept.

And now, I was sure, I never would.

I was not foolish enough to believe that I could take on Visser Three and survive. Maybe if I planned well, and was lucky, I might get him. But I would never live to brag about it.

Probably it was just as well. I had no future.

Lirem had "forgiven" me for breaking the law. But I could never be a warrior now, let alone a prince. I would never be another Elfangor. He would go down in history as a great hero. I would be remembered as the young, stupid little brother who gave the humans the ability to morph.

I had to morph into a human to go to the barn. There was always the chance that Cassie's father or mother might walk in.

But I felt bad assuming the human body. As the human skin replaced my own fur, and human eyes took over for my Andalite eyes, I kept remembering Lirem talking about how he had been an advisor to the Hork-Bajir.

The Hork-Bajir had lost. The Yeerks had enslaved them. But Lirem had been true to the laws and the customs.

What if he hadn't? What if he had given the Hork-Bajir advanced technologies? What if he had taught the Hork-Bajir to build spaceships? Would the Hork-Bajir still be a free people today?

It wasn't for me to decide. I was just an *aristh*. I would never be anything more. At least if I destroyed Visser Three, people would say, <He was a fool, but in the end he died well.>

Somehow that was *not* a great comfort.

I found the others already waiting inside the barn. Prince Jake was sitting on a bale of hay. Marco leaned against a stall, standing with arms crossed. Cassie, as usual, kept busy, feeding an injured baby goose with an eyedropper. Rachel paced back and forth, her cool eyes narrowing as she noticed me.

And Tobias . . . Tobias perched in the rafters overhead. I met his intense, intimidating hawk's gaze. And I saw that from his talons there hung a strip of bloody cloth. I knew where it had come from. And now I knew the reason for this meeting.

"Hi, Ax," Prince Jake said. "How's it going?"

"I'm fine," I answered.

"I figured we should all get together," Prince Jake said wearily. He seemed to be averting his eyes from me. "We need to think about what this thing with the Controllers means. We saw the guy at the mall. Then there was Mr. Pardue. And in the paper this morning there was a story about some guy, some business guy, who's in a meeting and freaks out. The paper made it seem like he just went nuts. I'm pretty sure he was another Controller losing it."

He looked at me. I said nothing.

"See, it's like this, Ax," Marco said suddenly. "We're tired of you giving us a runaround. Tobias shows up and he's dragging around some bloody shirt. I ask him what it is, and he won't tell me. Why won't Tobias tell me? Simple. He must have promised someone he wouldn't. And who would that someone be?"

There was no point denying it. "I made Tobias promise. Puh-romise. It is my fault."

"So now you're not just keeping secrets from us, you're getting us to keep secrets from ourselves!" Rachel yelled. "You need to get something straight, Ax. We're not your little action figures here. We're not toy soldiers. This is our planet. And this is our fight. You don't control us, just because you're some *mighty* Andalite."

"I am not trying to control anyone," I said.

"Yeah, right!" Rachel snapped. "The information all goes one way. We tell you everything, you tell us squat. Oh, you sound like you're being straight sometimes, but you never tell us anything useful."

"You said you knew the Yeerks would probably destroy any Controller that went bad on them," Marco pressed. "How did you know that? Has all this happened before, on some other planet?"

Rachel took over. "We show you our world. We take you in. You see our families, you read our books, you even go to our school. And then you keep secrets from us."

I felt battered by their words. They were all true. But I had my orders. I had the laws of my people.

"We're inferior, aren't we?" Marco said. "That's it, right? We're not good enough. Backward little humans. We don't deserve to be treated like equals."

"That's not it," I said.

"Sure it is!" Marco yelled. "Sure it is! We're just some bunch of cavemen, aren't we? That's what we look like to you."

Maybe I would have done better if I had been in my own body. My human body was awash in adrenalin. I was frustrated and afraid and guilty. "I can't answer your questions!" I yelled. "I can't!"

"You mean, you *won't*!" Marco yelled. "Rachel's right. We're just pawns in the big game. It's Andalites versus Yeerks in the big game and we're what? The towel boys?"

"Look . . . look . . . I have to follow the rules."

"Do you?" Cassie asked. It was the first time she had spoken. Her voice was soft and reasonable. "Did Elfangor follow the rules when he gave us the power to morph?"

"I'm *not* Elfangor!" I yelled. "Can't you see that? I'm not some big hero. I'm just a young Andalite, all right? You want the truth? Here's some truth for you: I'm not a warrior. I'm an *aristh*. A . . . a trainee. A cadet. A nobody."

"Yeah, yeah, boo-hoo," Marco sneered. "I'm not impressed. We don't want your sad story, we want the truth. What were you and Tobias doing? Why did you swear him to secrecy? What's going on?"

"I can't tell you," I said softly. "There's a law against giving aliens . . . I mean, any non-Andalite . . . our technology. And part of that law is we can't explain why. Can't. Tuh. Can't."

"I am sick of this from —" Rachel started to raise her voice to me again, but Prince Jake stood up and took her arm. I saw him look at Cassie. Cassie nodded.

"I can almost understand the part about not giving us advanced technology," Prince Jake said. "But why all the other secrets? Why can't you tell us other things, like how you knew what the Yeerks would do? Okay, so you don't want to give us megaweapons or whatever. Fair enough.

But to refuse even to tell us how we fit into this whole Yeerk – Andalite war? I mean, what's that about?"

"It's about keeping control of us," Marco said.

"It's about power," Rachel agreed.

Cassie was looking at me strangely. "No," she said. "That's not it. It's not about control. It's about guilt. Shame. That's it, isn't it? That's what you said the other night. You said every species carries some guilt."

"Guilt? Shame?" Marco asked, looking at Cassie like she was foolish.

But Cassie had found the truth.

"What did you guys do to be ashamed of?" Prince Jake asked me.

"Once we were kind when we should not have been kind," I answered.

"And that's all you're going to tell us?" Prince Jake asked.

I nodded, the way humans do.

"I can't accept that, Ax," Prince Jake said sadly. "If you're with us, you have to be honest with us. Otherwise . . . I guess you'll have to be on your own. I hate to do that. But you can't be one of us and then lie to us."

"I understand," I said. "You have been . . ." Once again, I was feeling that strange choking in my throat. "You've been very wonderful to me. I will always be grateful. Wonderful. Grateful. Ful. The truth is . . . the truth is we would not have been together much longer anyway."

I looked up at Tobias. Only he knew what I meant.

Slowly, feeling as if my clumsy human legs were made of a heavy Earth metal called lead, I turned and walked away from my human friends.

CHAPTER 18

"You can't always get what you want. But if you try sometimes, you just might find, you get what you need." A famous human named Rolling Stones said that. I thought it was very wise, for a human.
— From the Earth Diary of Aximili-Esgarrouth-Isthill

The morning ritual is for normal times. The next morning was not a normal time.

This was the day I would die.

<I am the servant of the people,> I said, and bowed my head low.

The people! The people were billions of miles away.

<I am the servant of my prince,> I said, and raised my stalk eyes to the sky.

My prince? Elfangor had been my prince. He was dead. Now a human, Jake, was my prince, and he had discharged me. I wasn't even telling him what I was doing.

The ritual was a lie.

<I am the servant of honor,> I said, and raised my face to look at the rising sun.

Honor. To die avenging my brother. I felt my insides quiver. It was fear. I know fear. I've felt it often enough in battle. But I'd never gone into a fight I *knew* I would lose.

This wasn't honor. It was running into the hands of death.

<My life is not my own, when the people have need of it.>

Couldn't I ask the others for help? Couldn't I go to Prince Jake and tell him?

No. Not without telling them that I had called my home world. Not without agreeing to tell them everything.

It was time for the last words of the ritual.

<My life . . . is given for the people, for my prince, and for my honor.>

I drew up my tail blade and pressed it against my throat in the symbol of self-sacrifice. I was breathing hard, as if I'd just been running. My hearts were beating fast.

<That's different,> Tobias's voice said. <That's not the ritual you were doing the other day. You didn't step into the water this time.>

<Yes. Different,> I muttered. I was angry that Tobias was there.

<You're going to do this, aren't you?>

131

I didn't answer. The truth was, I couldn't stand to talk about it. I was afraid. Sickly afraid. If I could achieve surprise, maybe I could kill the Visser. But he had the body of an Andalite adult. A full-grown male. The Visser was also more experienced than I was. And he would have guards. There would be Hork-Bajir nearby.

<Kind of cold-blooded, isn't it?> Tobias asked. <I mean, it's one thing in a battle. But just setting out to assassinate someone —>

<*Assassinate?!*> I yelled. <He killed my brother! He has humans infested by the handful. He will destroy you all if he can. He will enslave your entire race.>

<I wasn't criticizing. I'm a predator myself. But you could use some help. Tell me where it's happening, Ax. Tell me where you're going to find him. The others will help. You know they will.>

<I can't. I can't ask for help. Jake is my prince now . . . or was . . . he might forbid me.>

<Wait a minute. You mean Jake could just tell you no, and you wouldn't do it? What if he ordered you to answer all our questions? Then what?>

<Everyone must have someone over him. That is Andalite custom. Each warrior has a prince. Each prince a war-prince. Each war-prince has a great leader. And each great leader must be elected by the people as a whole. And everyone,

no matter how great or small, obeys the law. He could not order me to break our laws.>

<And Jake is your prince. I guess he's mine, too, in a way. You know, he doesn't think of himself that way.>

<No he doesn't. I realize this.>

<Don't you have a duty to tell your prince what you're doing?>

<Yes. So I guess I'm not very good at being a true warrior,> I said bitterly. <I'm not much good at anything.>

<I don't think that's true,> Tobias said.

<Tobias? I have to do this. You promised to keep my secret. Will you break your promise?>

Tobias said nothing for a while. <I won't tell anyone,> he said at last.

<And you won't follow me?>

<I won't follow you,> Tobias said.

<After . . . I mean, if I don't return. Just in case. Tell the others that . . . that I'm sorry I could never tell them everything. There is a reason.>

<Yeah, no doubt,> Tobias said bitterly. <Well, good luck, Ax-man.>

I ran then. I ran and ran and ran.

It was miles to the secret place where I would find Visser Three. I wanted to run the whole way, to run away from my own fear by heading straight toward it.

It's what Elfangor would have done. Elfangor, the great hero.

Elfangor would live on in everyone's memory as the perfect warrior. The shining prince. If I was lucky, someday people would say, <Ah, yes, Aximili broke the law, but he finished off the Abomination.>

I would get points for that. People would say I had done well in the end. Others would say, <What other choice did he have? He was dishonored. It wasn't courage that sent him against Visser Three, it was merely despair.>

And still others would say, <He was just a young fool trying to live up to his great brother's legacy, poor thing.>

I ran and ran till my chest ached from breathing the heavy air of Earth. I ran through dried leaves and rustling pine needles. I jumped fallen, rotting logs, and skirted patches of brambles. I ran past trees that did not speak, like the trees of my own world.

Each time I pictured being face-to-face with Visser Three, I went even faster, trying to outrun the fear.

I was far from any human homes now. Far from human roads. Deep within the forest. Old forest full of shadows and gloom.

But at last I saw the sun shining on green

grass, just ahead. A meadow. Right where Eslin's note had said it would be.

I stopped running and gasped for breath. I leaned against a tree and tried to recover my wind. My legs were shaking from a mixture of exhaustion and fear.

The meadow was beautiful. Green grass and tiny flowers in yellow and purple. I would have liked to feed there myself.

I crept toward the meadow's edge, always keeping within the shadow of the trees. I saw nothing unusual. No Bug fighters. No Hork-Bajir. No Visser Three.

Just the wildlife of Earth: two deer grazing. Squirrels racing up and down the trunks of trees. A skunk waddling boldly past.

It would be an hour before the time the Yeerk Eslin had given me. I had an hour to plan and prepare, now that I saw the ground we were on.

I looked at the meadow. A stream, perhaps three feet across, cut the meadow in half. The grass grew tall by the stream bed.

I tried to guess where the Visser would run. Would he go to the left or the right? I would only get one chance, so I had to guess right.

I imagined where I would go, if it were me. Visser Three was in an Andalite body. Maybe he would move like an Andalite.

135

I stepped out into the blazing sunlight and walked to a place I thought would do. It was beside the small stream. A place where the grass was a bit shorter, and where it would be easy for Visser Three to step into the stream.

Then, I saw them: the hoofprints. Andalite hoofprints.

Visser Three. Yes, he had been there, perhaps a few days earlier. Eslin was right. This was the place.

I had to wait, concealed. Ready to attack at the right time. I could never hide in my Andalite body. But there were other options.

The rattlesnake. That would be the morph to use. What better way to strike suddenly than with the body of a snake?

I focused my mind on the snake. I concentrated on the change. I felt it begin almost immediately.

It was unlike any morph I had done before. Usually my legs would become some other type of leg. My arms would become some other type of arm, even if they were only fins.

But this time there were no arms, no legs. Nothing of my own body would find an echo in this new shape, except for my eyes and tail.

My legs simply melted away. Withered. Disappeared. I fell to the ground, a legless stump.

My arms shriveled and evaporated.

I heard the sounds of grinding inside my body, as all my bones melted together into my spine.

I was shrinking, but since I was already lying on the grass, it didn't seem as extreme as it sometimes did. The stalks of grass grew higher around my head, and the purple flowers grew larger, but there wasn't the usual feeling of falling as I shrank.

What I did feel was a terrible sense of utter weakness. I had no arms! I had no legs!

But my tail . . . ah, that I kept, although in a very different form. The blade of my tail suddenly broke up into a sort of chain. There were dozens of raspy blisters, all connected. The rattler's tail.

My fur disappeared very swiftly, and over my bare skin scales grew. Like tiny, interlocked armor-plates that formed a pattern in brown and black and tan.

I grew a mouth. A huge mouth for the size of my body. I was a tube, and the open end was my mouth. It was a shocking body. A bizarre body. Stranger even than morphing an ant or a fish. I was a creature with no separate parts.

My Andalite stalk eyes went dark. A large, amazingly long, fast-moving, forked tongue grew in my mouth. But it wasn't like a human tongue.

137

This tongue's sense of taste was beyond anything a human tongue could ever achieve. This tongue tasted the very air.

And then, I felt the feature I had waited for. Huge, long, curved fangs. Fangs that were each a tiny, hollow needle. Above them poison glands grew and filled with toxin.

I felt the snake's mind emerge beneath my own awareness.

It was not a hot, driven mind like some animals. It did not overwhelm me with fear and hunger. It was a slow, calm, deliberate mind. The mind of a predator. A hunter. A calm, deliberate killer.

And the senses!

The lidless eyes saw strange colors, but they gave me a good range of vision.

The tongue, which shot out from a slit on the bottom of my mouth, taste-smelled the air. It brought me an incredible array of sensations: the scent of grass and earth, the scent of insects, and the scent of living, warm-blooded creatures.

Just below and behind my snake nostrils were two pits that sensed heat, especially the levels of heat put off by prey.

Yes, this was a good morph to use. The Visser would not expect me. The Visser's Andalite body was fast, but it was not faster than the snake. I knew that from my own experience.

I began to move, slithering through the grass. I moved with sinuous grace, easily, silently. I followed my tongue. It shot out and back, again and again, sensing, smelling, tasting.

I felt the rattler's mind with my own. It was unafraid. It had no honor. It had no friends to worry about, no family to disappoint, no laws to break. It felt no loneliness. The snake had always been alone.

I settled into the grass and waited, patient, motionless, counting off the minutes in my head.

And then I felt the vibration of the earth beneath me. The vibration that was the sound of a Bug fighter landing. Then another. Just two. Not far away.

It was time.

The Yeerks were coming. Visser Three was coming.

And as I drowned my fear in the calm lake of the snake's predator brain, I prepared to kill.

And to die.

CHAPTER 19

I smelled him long before I saw him. I smelled Andalite flesh. The Yeerk that was the real Visser Three — the Yeerk inside the Andalite body — I could not smell.

<Spread out,> Visser Three ordered. His thought-speech was loud, open, to reach his soldiers. <You! Watch the tree line. You two to the far side of the meadow. Shoot anything that moves.>

His voice was in my head. I felt churning in a stomach I no longer really had. I tried to squash my own fear beneath the snake's calm, but it rose suddenly.

I went over the plan: strike, escape, demorph, go back for the kill.

I would have to demorph before the Visser's guards could come to his side. And I would have to hope that the snake venom would slow him down.

Then . . . galloping!

Four sharp hooves beating across the meadow. My tongue flicked and smelled him on the wind.

Yes. He was coming closer.

Yes, he would come to the stream.

A shadow. He was there! Overhead. He blotted out the sun.

My snake tongue smell-tasted him. My lidless, always-open eyes saw his belly overhead like a curved roof. I felt his warmth.

He stuck one hoof into the cool water to drink.

No time to think. He could move at any moment.

T-S-S-S-S-S-S-S-S!

A sound! What was it?

Me! It was coming from me! My tail!

A rattlesnake's tail! It had sounded its grim warning without conscious thought.

I saw the Visser's head lowered. I saw his two main eyes focus. I could read the dawning fear in his eyes.

SSSSSS-ZAAPP!

I struck! My coiled muscles fired all at once.

141

My head rocketed through the air. My mouth opened wide. My fangs came down.

STRIKE!

Fangs sank deep into Andalite flesh. I could feel the venom pumping! I could feel the poison shooting into Visser Three's leg.

He jerked.

I released.

He tried to back away. He was very fast. But I was so much faster.

STRIKE!

Pump the venom into him. Poison the monster. Poison the Abomination. Poison Elfangor's murderer.

I drew back. I could taste my own venom dripping from my fangs.

His tail swept over his head, lancing down at me.

But I was already gone. The blade sliced deep into the ground. I felt the wind of it as I slithered swiftly away.

<DEMORPH!> I ordered myself.

Still the Visser had not called his guards. He would be wondering. He wouldn't know how dangerous the snake was. He wouldn't realize at first that it was not a true snake. Then slowly he would begin to suspect.

I was racing at breakneck speed through the

grass. Behind me my rope body twisted and coiled and released and slithered. But my head stayed level and straight, flying at ground level through the grass.

I was twenty yards away when my snake body grew slow and sluggish from the changes. Tiny legs appeared, just stubs at first. Tiny stalk eyes grew from the broad top of my diamond-shaped head.

<There is a snake!> Visser Three roared. <Find it! Kill it!>

I struggled on, heading for the edge of the forest.

Then . . . body warmth! A warm-blooded animal. Just ahead of me.

My tongue flicked and smelled an aroma I knew. Hork-Bajir!

Hork-Bajir, the shock troops of the Yeerk empire. A peaceful, decent race that happened, as Marco often said, to be built like lawn mowers. Bladed arms. Bladed legs. Tearing, clawed feet. A slow but deadly tail. They were all Controllers. All slaves of the Yeerks in their heads.

I could move no further. I was no longer a snake. Not yet an Andalite. And the Hork-Bajir was just a few feet away.

Too close!

<So,> I thought,<this is how it all ends.>

My Andalite stalk eyes had emerged. I was rising slowly from the grass on my spindly Andalite legs. My tail was forming again.

I saw the Hork-Bajir. And I saw that he saw me.

There was nothing I could do. Nothing I could do but die.

The Hork-Bajir swung his bladed right arm like a scythe. It would hit me in the neck.

WHUMPH! The Hork-Bajir staggered. His blade arm sliced the air above me.

"HhhhhuuuurrrrrOOOOWWWWRRR!" A roar! But not the roar of a Hork-Bajir.

The Hork-Bajir went flying! Seven feet of deadly, dangerous Hork-Bajir warrior just cartwheeled through the air.

And where he had been now stood Rachel.

Of course, not the human Rachel with long blond hair and cool blue eyes. This was another Rachel. Rachel in the morph of a grizzly bear.

The bear was on its hind legs, standing even taller than the Hork-Bajir had stood. With claws that almost rivaled the Hork-Bajir's blades. And muscles powerful enough to simply throw a Hork-Bajir ten feet.

"HHHHuurrhhoooorrwww!" the bear growled wildly. <Oh, man, I love doing that!>

<Rachel?> I asked wonderingly.

<No,> she said, in that human tone that means sarcasm. <It's Smokey the Bear. Finish morphing, you Andalite idiot. Then let's go kick some Yeerk butt.>

I was almost fully Andalite again. I swept the meadow quickly with my stalk eyes. Visser Three was in the middle of the field. Two Hork-Bajir were rushing to his side, bounding through the grass.

Across the meadow at the far end, a third Hork-Bajir looked around wildly, with his Dracon beam at the ready. He looked in every direction but up.

From the tree above him something that seemed almost liquid, something orange and black, dropped, claws outstretched.

Prince Jake!

And in the sky overhead, a hawk wheeled in low circles above the field.

<Two Hork-Bajir guarding the Bug fighters,> Tobias announced. <One Hork-Bajir in the . . . Oh, never mind, Cassie and Marco just took him down. Visser Three and two Hork-Bajir in the center of the meadow.>

<Come on,> Rachel said to me. <Let's go have a nice talk with Visser Three.>

<He's *my* responsibility,> I said to Rachel. <I have an obligation of honor.>

145

<Uh-huh. He's all yours.>

Tobias swooped past, skimming just above the grass, rocketing toward Visser Three.

<You told them, Tobias,> I accused him.

<Yeah, I sure did. I got the idea from you. You're the one who said you had to obey your prince. Well, I guess Jake is my prince, too. He ordered me to tell him.>

<How did you know where I was going?> I asked. <I never told you.>

<Puh-leeze. That Controller, Eslin Whatever? He wrote it down, Ax-man. You forget: I have hawk's eyes. I can see a flea on a cat from a hundred feet away. You think I couldn't read that note?>

<You make me very angry, Tobias,> I said.

<Yeah, and you get on my nerves, too, Ax. But we still have a fight on our hands. Let's go deal with Visser Three.>

We raced toward the Visser and his guards. Rachel, a huge, rolling brown tidal wave, and me. Above us Tobias flew.

Just as we drew close, I saw Visser Three stagger.

The poison! The venom! It was working.

Visser Three buckled and fell to the ground.

The two Hork-Bajir quailed. They saw Rachel barreling through the tall grass. They saw Prince Jake, a striped demon coming from the other side. They saw Marco in gorilla morph and Cassie, an eager wolf, teeth bared.

Tobias had reached the Visser. He soared past him and up, up, up into the air, beating frantically.

Worst of all, they saw an Andalite. The enemy they feared most.

<Your Visser is finished,> I called to them. <You can die with him, or you can run.>

The Hork-Bajir Controllers made their decision quickly. Hork-Bajir can be very fast, once they decide to run.

The Visser was down. Alone. Helpless, as we came to a stop in a circle around him. He was as helpless as Elfangor had been at the end.

I looked up. Why was Tobias . . . ?

<No way!> Tobias cried.

He drew back his wings and dived at full speed. He plummeted toward the earth at racing speed, killing speed! His talons came forward. It looked as if he would hit the ground. Then . . .

<NO! NO! NO!> Tobias cried. He swooped up and away, back up into the sky.

<Tobias, what is it?> I heard Prince Jake yell in thought-speak.

<He bailed! He bailed! The Yeerk bailed out! He got to the water. I can't see him. He got away!>

<What?> I cried. <What happened?>

147

<He's out! Visser Three! He's out. I saw him worming his way through the grass.>

It took several seconds for my brain to comprehend. I couldn't make sense of it. It was impossible to believe.

<He left his body?> I asked. <Visser Three left his host?>

<He crawled right out of the Andalite head and slithered into the water,> Tobias confirmed. <There's a fast current. I can't see beneath the surface of the water that well. I can't see him!>

I looked down at the creature I thought of as Visser Three. But of course the real Visser was a gray slug, a Yeerk. This body was the body of an Andalite.

The Visser was gone. Escaped.

The Andalite was breathing, but seemed unable to move. He looked up at me with his main eyes.

I had faced Visser Three before. I had felt the evil force that flows from him. That evil was gone now. This was only an Andalite. The Yeerk was gone.

<Kill me,> the Andalite managed to gasp. <Kill me before he takes me over again. Please. Please kill me.>

I felt my hearts stop. It was more than I could stand. After years of being controlled by Visser Three, the mind of the Andalite host was still alive. Still aware. <I may already have killed you, my friend,> I said. <The snake . . .>

<No. You don't understand. Visser Three . . . he has backup forces ready. They'll be here in minutes. Half a dozen Bug fighters. They'll keep this body alive, your poison is too slow.>

<I . . . but you're an Andalite. I can't kill you,> I said desperately. <I can't . . .>

<He'll take me again,> the Andalite said, begging. <The Yeerks will find him and bring me to him again. Please. I can't live that way . . . please. The things I've seen . . . you don't understand. It's horrible.>

He tried to raise his own Andalite tail. He tried to bring the blade to his throat. But the venom had weakened him. His tail fell limp.

<I understand,> he said at last, with sadness so deep it burned me to hear. <Listen . . . my name is . . . what is my name? It's been so long. And the poison . . . yes, that's it. My name is Alloran-Semitur-Corrass. I was once a war-prince. Someday . . . someday, if you survive . . . I have a wife. I have two children . . . someday . . . tell them I still hope . . . tell them I still have love for them . . .>

<Yes, War-Prince Alloran. I will tell them. Do you have any other orders for me?>

He reached up with one weakened hand. I took his hand in mine. <Fight them. They are

149

stronger than you think. They have . . . they have infiltrated . . . they are on the home world . . . fight . . .>

His fingers were limp. He fell silent, unconscious.

I set his hand down by his side. I knew that the next time I saw this face, it would once more be the face of my enemy. The Abomination. Visser Three.

<We should get out of here,> Prince Jake said.

<Come on, Ax,> Tobias said. <There will be another time.>

CHAPTER 20

> "Give me liberty or give me death." A human named Patrick Henry said that. I wonder if the Yeerks knew before they came to conquer Earth that humans said things like that. I wonder if the Yeerks knew what they were getting into.
> — From the Earth Diary of Aximili-Esgarrouth-Isthill

<We call it the law of *Seerow's Kindness*,> I said.

We were in the woods where I live. The woods of the planet called Earth.

Two days had passed since the terrible events in the meadow. I had thought a great deal in those two days. I had thought about everything. Then I had asked my human friends if they would join me.

"What's it mean?" Rachel asked.

She was standing with her arms crossed. I believe it was an expression of skepticism.

151

<It means that we are not allowed to transfer advanced technology to any other race,> I explained. <It is a very important law. One of our most important laws.>

"You don't want any competition," Marco said. "You Andalites want to be able to stay on top. I understand that. But humans are on your side. We're the ones being taken over."

"Marco," Prince Jake said. "Chill. Let Ax tell his own story."

<Seerow was a great Andalite. A warrior. A scientist. He . . . he was in charge of the first Andalite expedition to the Yeerk home world.>

I saw my human friends stiffen. Tobias flitted to a lower branch, drawing closer.

<Seerow felt sorry for the Yeerks. They were an intelligent species. They used a primitive species called Gedds as hosts. But the Gedds were nearly blind, clumsy, not very useful. The Yeerks had never even seen the stars. Let alone been able to leave their own planet. Seerow felt sorry for them. Seerow was a kind, decent Andalite . . .>

"Oh my God," Cassie whispered. "That's the big secret. That's the shame the Andalites are hiding."

"What?" Rachel asked. "What's the big secret?"

"Seerow gave the Yeerks advanced technology, didn't he?" Cassie asked.

I nodded. <Seerow thought the Yeerks should be able to travel to the stars, as we did. At first, it seemed like the right thing to do. But then . . . a species called the Nahara. . . . By the time we found out, it was too late. The entire species was enslaved by the Yeerks. Then came the Hork-Bajir. The Taxxons. And other planets . . . other races were falling to the Yeerk empire. They spread like a disease! Millions . . . billions of free people have been enslaved or destroyed by the Yeerks. Because of Seerow. Because of us. Because of the Andalites.>

For a while no one spoke. I knew what to expect. These humans had first seen Andalites as heroes. Then they had come to be suspicious. Now I had just confirmed their suspicions. Now they would see that Andalites were not the great saviors of the galaxy.

"Elfangor broke the law of *Seerow's Kindness*, though, right?" Marco pointed out.

<Yes. But I will take the blame for him. Elfangor was a great hero. His name would be destroyed. I'm a nobody. I have taken the blame. If I help you, and you humans become a new race of conquerors, if you become the new Yeerks some day, my people will talk about *Aximili's Kindness*. And I'll be the one who goes down in history as the new example of a fool.>

I saw Rachel make a small smile and shake

her head. Marco rolled his eyes. He said, "Man, and I really was getting into disliking you, Ax."

I was confused. I expected them to be furious. Instead they were each smiling.

<Don't you understand? Your world is threatened by the Yeerks because of my people.>

Prince Jake nodded. "Yes, we understand, Ax. A long time ago someone tried to be nice and it was a disaster. This Seerow person tried to be a good guy. He hoped all the different people of the galaxy would get along. That we'd all go to the stars together."

<Yes, and the result was terrible.>

"Ax, you don't stop hoping just because it doesn't always work out," Cassie said. "You get more careful. You get wiser, maybe. But you keep hoping."

"Look, Ax," Prince Jake said, "we don't want you to give us any Andalite technology. We don't want you to break your laws. We just want you to trust us. Tell us the truth. Be one of us."

"You aren't alone, Ax," Cassie said softly. "Maybe we aren't your people, but we are your friends."

"Your boy Seerow wasn't wrong," Marco said. "He just hooked up with the wrong species. We aren't the Yeerks. We're Homo sapiens, jack. Humans. Andalites want someone to cruise the stars with them? We're the ones. You bring the spaceships. We'll bring the Raisinets and cinnamon buns."

<You'll do more than that,> I said. <You learn very quickly. Someday you may be greater than the Andalites.>

"No," Prince Jake said. "Because whatever we learn, you'll learn. We'll do it together. Human and Andalite. Andalite and human."

<It isn't possible,> I said. <We are two different species. From two different worlds, a billion Earth miles apart.>

<Ax-man?> Tobias said. <Tell me: What does an Andalite want most? What is it you guys are fighting for?>

<For freedom, of course,> I said.

<And what do humans want most?> Tobias asked.

"Freedom," Prince Jake said.

"Freedom," Rachel said, nodding her head.

"Freedom," said Marco and Cassie together.

<Freedom,> Tobias said. <Different bodies, different species, maybe. But who cares? We agree on what matters.>

For a few minutes, I said nothing. I guess I felt a little overwhelmed. Then, I realized something that made me laugh. <See? It's happening already,> I said.

"What?" Rachel asked.

<You humans are already teaching Andalites

155

something new,> I said. <You're right. We fight the same battle, for the same goal.>

"The Andalites on your home world may not like that idea," Rachel said.

<No. They won't. They have their laws and customs. They think they know what's right. If I ever go home, I'll have a lot to explain.>

<Maybe so,> Tobias said. <But I know one Andalite who would have been proud of you.>

"Are you with us?" Prince Jake asked.

<Yes, Prince Jake,> I said.

"Don't call me 'Prince.'"

<Yes, Prince Jake,> I said again.

"All right," Marco said, rubbing his hands together. "Now that's over with. And now that we are finally all leveling and telling the truth . . . I think we have one very big question for Ax. One huge question that will put our new friendship to the test. One gigantic question."

Everyone nodded in agreement.

<What?> I asked nervously.

"How, how, HOW do you eat without a mouth?" Marco demanded.

I laughed. <We eat as we run. Our hooves crush the grass, and the nutrients are absorbed into our systems. We drink in the same way, by putting a hoof into water.>

<Ahhh, so that's what the whole thing is with

the morning ritual, when you stick a hoof in the water,> Tobias said.

"Morning ritual? What morning ritual?" Rachel asked.

"Yeah, tell us," Cassie said.

<Okay,> I agreed. <I will tell you everything. Everything I know.>

I looked directly at Tobias as I said that. I met his fierce, intense hawk's gaze. I wanted him to understand that I would answer *his* question as well. The question I knew must be burning inside him.

But the question never came. And I heard in my mind an echo of Tobias's words. <Different bodies, different species, maybe. But who cares? We agree on what matters.>

Neither I, nor my *shorm* Tobias, is capable of smiling. But just the same, there are times when we look at each other, and understand each other, and smile.

CHAPTER 21

<You'll do it because if you don't, I'll find a way to tell Visser Three who set him up,> I told Eslin, the Yeerk traitor.

I was in the observatory. We were alone, just the two of us. Eslin glared hatefully at me.

"Andalite scum. You couldn't even kill the Visser. What's the matter? Did he scare you too badly?"

<Just boot up the software,> I said. <I have a transmission to make. This one time, Eslin, and I will be gone from your miserable life. Do it.>

It took several minutes for the Z-space transmission to be established. And it took a few moments more before I was connected to the great Lirem again.

<I won't be able to call again, most likely,> I said. <I have a message I need sent. To the wife of Alloran-Semitur-Corrass, from her husband.>

It was kind of nice to see old Lirem's eyes go wide all of a sudden. See, he knew exactly who Alloran was. *What* he was.

<Her husband sends his love. He still hopes for the day when he will be freed.>

<Is that all you have to say, *aristh* Aximili?>

<No . . . I have this to say, too. You tried to save the Hork-Bajir, and still live by all our laws. Still keeping all our secrets. But you failed.>

<Do not say what you are about to say, Aximili,> Lirem warned. <Do not disobey the laws of our people.>

<I . . . Prince Lirem, these humans are my people now. And, sir, with all due respect to the law and to you, I won't let the humans be destroyed as the Hork-Bajir were destroyed. Not while I live.>

Lirem's eyes narrowed dangerously. <It must run in your family,> he growled. <You're just like your brother, Elfangor.>

I laughed. <Thank you, Prince. Thank you very much.>

My termite body seemed to be moving on its own now. It was like I was a passenger in a car that someone else was driving.

<Is everyone through?> I asked.

<Yes,> Rachel said.

She sounded distracted to me. Like she was listening to someone else and didn't want me interrupting. But that was okay, because I didn't really want to talk to her, either.

I quickly covered the ground to the building. I didn't *see* that it was the building, you understand. I just knew. And the terrible thing is, I never even paused to wonder *how* I knew.

<What are we . . .> Marco's voice. He didn't finish his thought. I didn't care.

<Guys?> Rachel asked <Um . . .>

The opening was just ahead. I knew it was there. I knew that other soldier termites would be guarding the entrance.

I felt no fear.

I clambered up from the dirt into the tunnel opening. Familiar smells. Smells I knew. Home. Home. My place. Where I was from, and where I belonged.

I smelled the other soldiers with my antennae. They touched me with their antennae, as I did them. We were of the colony.

The colony.

I raced swiftly down the tunnel. It headed upward at a sharp angle, but the angle meant little to me. I weighed practically nothing. A worker was ahead of me. It extruded a pellet of digested cellulose. Wood pulp. I quickly gobbled it up.

Within the wood pulp food there were messages. Hormones passing through the colony, containing information. Vague orders. Indistinct yet powerful instructions.

I was now caught up in a rush of workers off to obey the voiceless voice in their heads. Some were off to chew a new tunnel. Others were off to the egg chamber to rotate the eggs.

And I had my orders, too.

I raced along tunnels lined with chewed and digested wood pulp. Tunnels cut through the dried wood that supported the building.

I felt side tunnels open on one side, then the next. A tunnel above. Air flowed faint — but fresh — actually creating a tiny breeze.

There was no light. None. But it didn't matter

because I was blind. I was blind, but I was not lost.

What am I doing? an alien voice asked.

I ignored it.

NO! the voice cried.

I had heard the voice before. But it came from far away and it spoke a language I didn't understand.

NO! NO! NO! Let me go!

I felt a queasy, sickening feeling inside me.

But still I powered down the tunnel, turning here, turning there. Always moving toward a goal. There was a powerful smell. It was growing stronger and stronger.

I went to it. I *had* to go to it.

NO! Let me go! Let me go!

Down the black tunnels. Over and through the packed rush-hour streams of workers. To the center. To the core. To the heart.

Help me! Help me! the voice screamed.

The voice . . . my voice.

The faint, failing voice of the human named Cassie.

Me.

Me!

Ahhhhhhhhh!

Suddenly, I was Cassie again. I knew my name. I knew who I was.

But it no longer mattered. The termite body

was out of my control. A stronger will than mine was guiding it.

The termite suddenly emerged into a vast, open space. A space that in reality was no more than two or three inches across. And yet it felt like an auditorium to me.

Suddenly I knew who had seized control of the termite brain.

I knew who had brushed my human mind aside.

She was vast. Huge beyond belief. At one end I sensed the termite head and useless, waving termite arms. From that small head and body there extended a monstrous, pulsating sack. As big as a blimp.

At the far end was a double row of sticky, slimy eggs, to be picked up and carried away by worker termites.

The queen.

I was in the chamber of the termite queen. . . .

COMING IN JULY

Visser Three has discovered a secret...
And the Animorphs have to move quickly —
before it's too late...

There's something pretty weird going on in the woods behind Cassie's house. The place where Ax and Tobias call home. It seems the Yeerks have figured out one very important thing: Andalites cannot survive without a feeding ground and if Visser Three finds Ax in the woods, nothing will stop him from finding the Animorphs...

ANIMORPHS #9: THE SECRET

K.A. Applegate

Visit the Web Site at: http://Scholastic.com/animorphs

JOIN US

ANIMORPHS™

K. A. Applegate

☐ BBP62977-8	**Animorphs #1: The Invasion**	$3.99
☐ BBP62978-6	**Animorphs #2: The Visitor**	$3.99
☐ BBP62979-4	**Animorphs #3: The Encounter**	$3.99
☐ BBP62980-8	**Animorphs #4: The Message**	$3.99
☐ BBP62981-6	**Animorphs #5: The Predator**	$3.99
☐ BBP62982-4	**Animorphs #6: The Capture**	$3.99
☐ BBP99726-2	**Animorphs #7: The Stranger**	$3.99
☐ BBP99728-9	**Animorphs #8: The Alien**	$3.99
☐ BBP21304-0	**Megamorphs #1: The Andalite's Gift**	$3.99

Available wherever you buy books, or use this order form.
Scholastic Inc., P.O. Box 7502, 2931 E. McCarty Street, Jefferson City, MO 65102

Please send me the books I have checked above. I am enclosing $ _____
(please add $2.00 to cover shipping and handling).
Send check or money order — no cash or C.O.D.s please.

Name _____ Birthdate _____

Address _____

City _____ State/Zip _____

Please allow four to six weeks for delivery. Offer good in U.S.A. only. Sorry, mail orders are not
available to residents of Canada. Prices subject to change.   ANI1296

Order your books. . .before it's too late!

WHAT DO YOU THINK?

ey you guys! We want to hear what you think about Animorphs. Just
nswer the questions below, fill in your name and address on the back of
is sheet, and send your survey back to us: **Animorphs Survey
:holastic Inc. 555 Broadway, New York, NY 10012-3999**. Thanks!

How did you first find out about Animorphs?

☐ School Book Club	☐ School Book Fair
☐ Local Bookstore	☐ Web
☐ friend/family	☐ TV commercial
☐ Library	☐ other_____

Who is your favorite character?

☐ Jake	☐ Rachel	☐ Tobias
☐ Cassie	☐ Marco	☐ Ax

Which of these characters do you like reading about most?

☐ Hork-Bajir	☐ Yeerks
☐ Taxxons	☐ Visser Three
☐ other_____	

Which is your favorite book?

☐ #1: The Invasion	☐ #5: The Predator
☐ #2: The Visitor	☐ #6: The Capture
☐ #3: The Encounter	☐ #7: The Stranger
☐ #4: The Message	

Which of these magazines do you like to read?

☐ Nickelodeon Magazine	☐ Girl
☐ SI for Kids	☐ Teen Beat
☐ Highlights	☐ YM
☐ Boys Life	☐ Sassy
☐ Other_____	

6) Which of these book series do you read?

☐ Goosebumps	☐ Sweet Valley Twins
☐ Baby-sitters Club	☐ other_____
☐ Fear Street	

7) Where did you get your most recent Animorphs book?

☐ School Book Club order	☐ School Book Fair
☐ Bookstore	☐ Supermarket
☐ School Library	☐ other_____
☐ Public Library	

8) How do you buy your Animorphs books?

☐ In numerical order
☐ Only the most recent titles
☐ Based on the cover design

9) Do you know about the Animorphs web site at http://www.scholastic.com/animorphs?

☐ Yes	☐ No

10) If so, how often do you visit the Animorphs web site?

☐ Never	☐ I hardly ever visit it
☐ Once a month	☐ Once a week
☐ Several times a week	☐ Almost everyday

11) How many Animorphs books have you read?_____

ANIMORPHS™

Now tell us about yourself!

☐ Boy ☐ Girl

Name _____ Birthdate _____

Mo./ Day/ Year

Address _____

City _____

State _____ Zip _____

Telephone ( ) _____ Grade _____